Jilted

Lexi Lawton

They've always been just friends—until now.

Brett Hudson and Amy King have been inseparable since childhood, their friendship surviving every twist life has thrown at them. But when Brett, a rising star on a popular TV dance show, falls for Vanessa—a glamorous costume designer—their bond faces its greatest test. In a whirlwind romance, Brett proposes. The catch? Vanessa demands he cut Amy out of his life forever.

Heartbroken, Amy watches as the man she secretly loves prepares to marry someone else. But when Vanessa leaves Brett at the altar, he turns to the one person who's always been there—Amy. Desperate to escape his humiliation, Brett invites Amy on his honeymoon, a week in paradise that promises sun, sand... and temptation.

When Brett suggests taking their friendship to the next level, Amy is torn. One passionate night could change everything, but if it goes wrong, she could lose him forever. Will they risk a lifetime of friendship for one night of passion?

A sizzling friends-to-lovers romance full of longing, heartbreak, and second chances.

Chapter One

Amy walked around the studio, double checking to make sure there was nothing on the floor. They'd been cleaned and freshly waxed two nights ago, and the studio had been closed to lessons all weekend, but the first class of the day was a group of fourteen- and fifteen-year-olds. They were a handful in their own right, but once the music got pumping, they were worse. Not to mention, at that age, the hormones were rampant.

She had several students who were here because they were serious about becoming professional ballroom dancers. Others, though, she was convinced they were just here to cop a feel with a member of the opposite sex. She remembered what it was like at that age. And she vividly remembered what it was like to dance with a boy she had a crush on.

Brett Hudson.

His name still gave her goose bumps.

Amy started dance classes when she was five. She met Brett when she was ten. They were paired up together during one lesson, and since that day, they've been dance partners, best friends, and now, they were business partners. Four years ago, they opened their own dance studio.

Satisfied that the floor was clean and safe, she moved on to make sure all the playlist was ready to go. Nothing disrupted the flow of a class more than having to stop and search for the correct music.

"I got it!" Brett rushed through the doors, his blue eyes sparkling. "I got it, Amy!"

"The TV show?" Amy exclaimed. "My God, Brett, that's fantastic. I'm so happy for you." She flung her arms around his neck and hugged him.

Brett picked her up, spun her around, and laughed. "I can't believe it either," he said, setting her back on her feet.

Amy couldn't keep the smile from her face. "Don't forget your friends when you become famous."

"Never." He dropped his bag on the floor and kicked it toward the corner. A habit of his that really annoyed her. "We have to go out and celebrate tonight."

"Yeah." She laughed. Since *Dancing Duel* had become so popular, Brett had joked about trying to become a professional dancer on the show. Amy had always encouraged him, but it wasn't until recently that he finally took her encouragement to heart. And now it had paid off. Big time. She was thrilled for him.

"We'll go to Gregorio's for dinner, and then to that new club on the boulevard for drinks and dancing." He snapped his fingers and wiggled his hips.

Amy laughed. "You mean Nefarious?"

"Yeah, that's the place. We'll go there and dance the night away."

Like they didn't dance enough as it was. She smiled and shook her head. It was a rare occasion to see Brett in such a good mood. He'd had a string of bad relationships lately, and they had taken a real toll on him emotionally. Getting on this show was exactly what he needed.

"I'll pick you up at six?"

"I'll be ready." She refocused her attention on the task at hand – getting the music ready for their upcoming class. "Oh, and Brett, tonight's my treat. No arguments."

He grinned big enough to showcase his dimple. Amy had more than one fantasy about kissing that very dimple. She looked away, afraid her true thoughts would be displayed on her face for him to see. Lying to him was something she never could successfully do.

In the entire time they'd known each other, not once had they ever shown any sort of sexual attraction to each other. No flirty looks or words; no drunken admissions of love; no regrettable caresses or kisses. They were just best friends and business partners. Plain and simple.

Of course, like any best friends they talked about everything, including relationships and sex. They just never talked about doing it together, even though she'd thought about it – a lot.

Why wouldn't she? He was tall, lean, and muscular, with abs to die for and arms that always kept her entranced. They were strong yet graceful. His legs were the same way, and she'd imagined more than once what it would feel like to have his svelte body pressed firmly against hers. Brett had a headful of thick, black hair, and piercing blue eyes.

Amy blew out a breath and fanned her face with her hand. She had to stop thinking about him like that. Nothing would ever come of it, and her inappropriate fantasies would only frustrate her.

"It is hot in here, isn't it?" Brett asked, interrupting her thoughts. "Is the air on?"

"Uh," she cleared her throat, "yeah, I think so. I'll go double check."

Amy quickly left the room, happy to be away from Brett for a few moments. What had gotten into her today? She hadn't thought of him like that in years. Why now? Why today?

She'd better get her act together before tonight because it would be a very long night if she spent it fantasizing about the one man she could never have.

"Is it just me or was that class more difficult than usual?" Brett blew out a breath and dragged a hand through his hair. "I don't know what got into them today, but damn." He laughed.

"It's spring. The kids are anxious for the nice weather. I guess it's to be expected." Amy sat in one of the chairs that were set out for the parents and removed the towel that she'd draped around her neck.

Next, she removed her heels. She rubbed the bottom of her foot. She extended her legs in front of her and wiggled her toes. That's when she noticed Brett staring at her, an odd look on his face.

"What?" she asked.

"Nothing." He shook his head. "Why do you keep wearing those shoes if they hurt your feet?"

"Because they're pretty." She smiled, and he laughed. "Once I break them in, they'll stop hurting."

"I'll never understand you women and your obsession with shoes."

"And I'll never understand you men and your obsession with throwing your stuff on the floor." She glanced toward the corner where he'd kicked his bag earlier.

He shrugged in typical Brett fashion – slow, lazy, and full of confidence. "At least it's out of the way."

Amy picked up her towel and threw it at him. "Would it really be so much trouble to just put it in the office?"

"I've got important stuff in that bag." He walked over and picked it up, putting the strap over his shoulder.

"What could you possibly have in there that you can't let it out of your sight for a single, fifty-minute lesson?"

"A man's duffel bag is like a woman's purse. Sacred and confusing."

She shook her head and smiled. "You are such a dork."

"Takes one to know one," he retorted with a smile.

Yeah, they were grown adults who still teased each other like kids. It was juvenile, but it was their thing, and she wouldn't change it for the world.

"Want to grab some lunch?" Brett asked.

"Yeah, it'll have to be quick though. I'm meeting with the realtor today." Amy picked up her heels and carried them into the back office. She slipped on her sandals and grabbed her purse.

"I forgot about that. Want me to go with you?" He stood in the doorway, arms crossed, looking perfectly at ease, perfectly sexy. Brett always wore a plain black T-shirt when teaching, and the fabric always stretched just right across his chest, showing the definition of his upper body.

Her gaze lingered longer than necessary on his muscular arms. What the heck was wrong with her today? Forcing herself to look away, she said, "Yeah, sure, if you want. All I'm doing is meeting with her to sign a contract and to give her an idea of the kind of space we're looking for."

Amy glanced around the office one final time to make sure she had everything; then she turned off the lights and followed Brett back into the studio.

"I think you forget sometimes that my name is on the sign out front, too." He gently nudged her shoulder. "We agreed that if we were going to open a second studio, we'd do it together. I want to help."

Amy could never forget that she and Brett were equal business partners, but she was the type of person who just naturally tried to do everything on her own. They needed another location, so she was doing what needed to be done to find it.

"Okay, if you want to spend this beautiful day going over a real estate contract, who am I to stop you?" she said with a shrug.

He laughed one of his deep, throaty laughs that always made her stomach drop to her feet and her heart flutter. "You're not getting rid of me that easily. Honestly, Amy, how long is this going to take? We'll be done and outside enjoying the sunshine in no time."

"You're a poet and didn't even know it." She playfully stuck her tongue out at him as they made their way to the parking lot.

"Who's the dork now?"

"I have learned from the best," she said, bowing at him as if he were royalty.

"Shut up and get in the car." He pointed his key fob at his car and pushed the unlock button.

Teaching dance lessons wasn't the highest paying profession, but no one would know that based on Brett's lifestyle. He drove a metallic blue Mercedes. It was a hot car, but very expensive. And his apartment was to die for. The view from his living room was breathtaking. He wouldn't live like he did if not for his hefty trust fund. But despite his money, he never acted like he was better than anyone else.

Amy, on the other hand, lived less extravagantly. Not because she couldn't afford to live like Brett – she could thanks to a large inheritance from her grandmother—but she preferred the simpler things in life. She owned her own house, a small, two-bedroom, one story Ranch outside of the city with a generous sized backyard. Someday, when she had children of her own, it would be the perfect place to raise them. And she drove a modest and safe SUV.

She opened the passenger's door and slid into the seat, loving how the cool leather felt against her bare legs. "So, where are you taking me to lunch?" Amy rested her elbow on the door and glanced at him.

"I don't recall offering to buy you lunch." Brett put the car in gear and pulled out of the parking lot.

"It's the least you can do considering I'm taking you out tonight." She kept her gaze on Brett, watching the way he concentrated on the road, the way the strong line of his jaw softened when he smiled, and then winked at her.

Amy wondered what it would feel like to nibble on his jaw. Good Lord, she had to get a grip. Seriously, what the hell was wrong with her today?

"Well, when you put it like that." He rolled his eyes. "Where do you want to go?"

"The realtor's office is over on Grant, so why don't we go to that new café on the corner of Thirty-one and Main?"

"Sounds good." Brett turned right onto the Boulevard and headed toward the other end of town.

Amy settled into her seat and relaxed. Her thoughts wandered to Brett's announcement from earlier. He was going to be on *Dancing Duel*. She truly was happy for him, but she knew that the show would keep him busy. They wouldn't have much time to just hang out. Her shoulders slumped with sadness. She would miss Brett. Miss them and the time they spend together.

Chapter Two

"Amy? Are you ready?" Brett shouted as he walked into her house without knocking.

That wasn't unusual for him. They both did it to the other. If, or when, they ever settled down, that kind of behavior would have to stop. Until then, he enjoyed the easy, relaxed nature of their friendship.

"Yeah, I'm ready." Amy walked out of her room dressed in a knee length purple dress that was cut low in the front.

The plunging neckline drew his gaze to her breasts. He'd seen her in a fair share of skimpy dance costumes that showed off her cleavage and her curves, but none of them had ever fazed him like seeing her in this dress did. Maybe because she wasn't in costume – she was just Amy— a sexy, gorgeous version of Amy that had him momentarily rethinking the whole platonic friendship thing. It wasn't the first time his thoughts had wandered down this forbidden path, but it was the first time his thoughts and feelings had been this strong.

"What?" she asked, smoothing her hands down her

stomach and hips. "Do I look bad? Is this dress too much? Should I go change?"

"No," he blurted out a little too quickly. "No, you look great."

"Then why are you staring at me like that?" She put her hands on her hips and glared at him.

Brett shook the inappropriate thoughts from his mind. Amy was his friend, his *best* friend, and sure, she was attractive as hell, but he was pretty sure she would laugh in his face if he ever told her how he really felt.

"I feel underdressed now," he said, waving his hands down the length of his body.

He'd dressed in a pair of navy-blue slacks, a black silk, button up shirt, and a cerulean-blue tie. Gregorio's was one of the fanciest Italian restaurants in the city, and there was a certain level of dress expected. He had no idea what kind of dress was normal or expected at the club. There were no doubts that Amy would fit right in, but he was starting to question his own wardrobe choice.

"You look fine, Brett. If anything, I'm overdressed."

He smiled as an inappropriate comeback about helping her become undressed popped into his mind. Brett shook the thoughts away. "Okay, so I'm underdressed, you're overdressed, and we're going to be late if we don't get going."

Amy laughed. She grabbed a shawl from the foyer closet, draped it around her shoulders, and said, "Let's get going then. I'm starving."

"Me too." Brett held out his arm, which Amy took, looping hers through his. He was looking forward to spending the evening with her.

Once outside, Brett opened the car door for her and helped her into the seat. As he made his way to the driver's side, he blew out a breath and tried to calm himself. His hands were shaking – friggin' shaking! He flexed his fingers several times before grabbing the door handle and getting in the car. The scent of Amy's perfume assaulted his senses. *Get a grip, Hudson!*

They were silent for a long while, which was unusual for them. It wasn't awkward, just a little weird. He kept glancing at her, hoping she didn't notice how strange he was acting. But damn...had Amy always been so hot?

His gaze dropped to her legs, and he devoured them with his eyes. Most men were either ass men or breast men. Brett was a leg man. And Amy had a great pair of legs. Long, slender, muscular. When he watched her dance, which he did a lot more than he cared to admit, he always focused on her legs. The way she moved, it was always so graceful, elegant...sexy.

"Brett?"

The sound of her voice snapped him from his thoughts. "What?"

She laughed. "You're a million miles away. What's up?"

He looked over at her and smiled. "Nothing, guess I'm just thinking about the show and everything I have to do."

"No." She turned in her seat and pointed at him. "No worrying about the show or the studio or anything else. We're here to have fun tonight. Got it?"

Brett laughed. "Yes, ma'am. Fun. Got it."

He pulled up in front of the restaurant and put the car in park. Getting out, he handed his keys to the valet, then walked around to Amy's side and opened her door. He took her hand and helped her out of the car.

"Thank you," she said as he escorted her inside.

Brett couldn't help but feel like he was on a date with Amy and that was just too weird. He had to shake this off or the night would be a bust. They were seated at a table in the back of the restaurant. Their waiter poured them a complimentary glass of white wine and left them to look at the menu.

"God, I'm so hungry I could eat a hippo on steroids," Amy said.

He laughed at her and all the awkward tension he felt disappeared. Just like that, Amy was simply Amy again, his best friend.

"Go crazy, you're paying." He winked at her over the menu, knowing full well that there was no way in hell he was letting her foot the bill for tonight.

Their waiter returned several moments later. "Are you ready to order?"

"Yes." Amy smiled. "I'll have the lobster Alfredo with a salad, light on the dressing please." She closed the menu and set it on the table. "Oh, and we'd like a bottle of Dom Perignon, too, please."

"And for you, sir?"

"I think I'm going to go with the steak Florentine," Brett said.

"Salad for you as well?" the waiter asked.

"Yes, please. No onion, extra dressing." The waiter nodded then left. Brett raised a brow at Amy. "Big spender tonight I see."

Dom Perignon was Amy's favorite champagne. It was also very pricey.

"It's not every day your best friend lands a job on the most popular television show. If this isn't a reason to spend frivolously, then what is?"

Brett shrugged and smiled. "You don't always need a reason to splurge, you know."

"No, but when you do, it makes it that much more fun."

Her big hazel eyes twinkled, and he was suddenly very

warm. He grabbed his glass of ice water and took a long drink. It was going to be a long night.

Brett stood at the crowded bar and waited, impatiently, for the bartender to acknowledge him. Amy was on the dance floor with a couple of women she'd met at the club tonight. She had a real knack for making friends wherever she went, which had paid off tonight because he'd spent more time waiting in line at the bar than he had dancing with her.

He looked around the club and let his gaze settle on Amy. Damn that woman knew how to move. He smiled as he watched her, but it quickly faded when he saw the group of men to her right. They were watching her, smiling, nodding, and acting like they were trying to get their long-haired friend to go talk to her. Sure enough, moments later, the hippie looking friend approached Amy.

Oh, hell no! Brett and Amy had one rule that they never broke: no picking up dates while they were out together. He'd be damned if he let some guy try to pick her up tonight. Leaving his place at the bar, Brett made his way toward Amy, reaching her the same time the other guy did.

Brett pulled Amy to him and started dancing with her. He gave the guy a dirty look that said, "Back off, she's taken."

Amy leaned forward and put her mouth near his ear. "I thought you were getting drinks."

"Line was too long." He spun her around and then pulled her to him again. Dancing with her like this, for fun, was so much better than dancing in a choreographed routine.

"Well, I need some water." Amy fanned her face with her hand and motioned for him to follow her.

He did, and they stood at the bar. Only this time, it didn't take so long to get a drink. They made their way toward an empty table in the corner.

"Phew." Amy plopped down in the seat and laughed. "Man, it's hot in here." She reached into her glass of water and grabbed a piece of ice, which she proceeded to rub around her neck and down her chest.

Brett's throat went dry watching her, watching the way she tilted her head back and closed her eyes, the way her lips were slightly parted as if suspended on a sigh of satisfaction. It stirred feelings in him that he shouldn't be feeling for his best friend.

He motioned for the waitress walking around with a tray of shots and bought four of them. Maybe if he consumed more alcohol, he wouldn't notice Amy so much, or at least if he did, he could pass it off on being drunk and not have to worry about the repercussions of ogling his best friend.

"Would you look at them?" Amy nodded to her right.

Brett followed the direction of her gaze to see a couple on the dance floor making out. The man had his hand on the woman's ass, her skirt bunched beneath his fingers. Her leg was bent at his waist, making it clear that she wasn't wearing any panties.

He downed one of his shots. "More power to 'em," Brett

finally said, drinking a second shot. It had been months since his last breakup and just as long since he'd had sex.

"Why can't we find significant others who are that hot for us?" Amy swirled her drink and then took a sip. "I mean, really, why are guys so intimidated by a strong, independent woman? Just because I have my life together and I know what I want doesn't mean I don't want a man to love me and take care of me."

Brett nodded. He'd heard this same thing from her every single time she broke up with a guy. And he knew how she felt. Every woman he'd ever been serious about always left him for one reason or another. Usually, it was because of Amy. Women were threatened by his close friendship with her. But he always refused to give her up despite repeated requests from his girlfriends. No way in hell. Amy had always been there, and she always would be.

Plus, other than a sister and a brother she didn't speak to, Amy didn't have any family. He was her family, and there was no way he could ever turn his back on her. Amy meant too much to him to just dump her because some woman he was dating wanted him too. Nope. Brett was resolved to the fact that either he would be single for the rest of his life, or he'd just have to wait a long time to find that special woman who would accept his friendship with Amy.

"It's because you go for the wrong type of guy," Brett said matter-of-factly, pouring a third shot down his throat. "Those muscle-bound jocks are all bark and no bite. They look good on the outside, but they're a mess on the inside."

Amy threw a piece of ice at him and laughed. "And the goody two shoes, schoolteacher types you date are much better?"

"Nope." He grinned. "Which is why we're both still single."

She sighed. "Yeah, so much for my dream of having kids."

"You're young. I'm sure you'll find someone." He drank his last shot and chased it with his beer.

"I'm thirty, Brett. By the time I find a man, date him, and get married, I'll be an old hag with no viable eggs."

The thought of Amy finding a man to marry and have kids with didn't sit well with him. He couldn't stomach the thought of losing her.

"I'll tell you what." He leaned across the table and pointed at her. "Three years from now, if neither of us are married, I'll marry you and give you as many babies as you want." Brett's words were slurred. Yup. He was definitely drunk. He wouldn't have made that proposition otherwise.

"Yeah right." Amy rolled her eyes. "You and me? That would be like fucking my brother. Thanks, but no thanks."

He flinched at her words. "You think of me as your brother?" That bothered him a lot more than it should, especially considering he'd never once thought of her as a sister.

She shrugged. "We're best friends. How else would I think of you?" Amy glanced away and then set her gaze on him again. "Why? How do you think of me?"

Oh shit! He hadn't expected the conversation to backfire on him like that. What was he supposed to tell her? That he thought of her as a best friend that he wanted to fuck? No, he definitely couldn't tell her that.

"As a friend, I guess. I don't know. It's not like I sit around and think about how I should think of you. You're Amy."

"And you're drunk."

"Maybe a little." He grinned. "So, do we have a deal or what?"

"Yeah, whatever. You're probably not going to remember this tomorrow anyway."

"Yes, I will," he insisted. "It's not every day I throw out marriage proposals y'know?"

"Okay then, you've got a deal." She smiled.

"You gotta shake on it." Brett extended his hand to her. She took it and gave it a firm shake. He smiled. Amy would always be around.

Chapter Three

Tonight was Thursday, which meant tacos from the corner food stand and really bad horror movies at the old Kalet theatre. It was what they did every Thursday night, but this week was extra special because tonight was Brett's last night at home. Tomorrow, he'd be boarding a plane to begin his work on *Dancing Duel,* and it would be months before they had a chance to hang out again. The thought really depressed her.

Amy sat across from him at the rickety, plastic table and watched as he licked taco sauce from the corner of his mouth. An unusually cool breeze blew over them, causing Amy's hair to blow into her face. She brushed it back and pulled it into a ponytail with the scrunchie she always wore on her wrist.

"Don't do that," Brett said, taking a sip of his soda.

"Don't do what?"

"Put your hair up like that." He crumpled his napkin and tossed it on their tray, which was now full of garbage.

She gave him an odd look. "It's blowing in my face." Standing, she gathered her purse and draped it over her shoulder. "Besides, since when do you care about my hairstyle?"

He shrugged in that cocky, sexy way he had about him and said, "I don't. But you wear it up all the time when you're teaching. It looks better down." He reached over and pulled the tie from her hair. "There." He smiled. "Much better."

What was up with him tonight? she wondered. He'd never once cared or mentioned her hair before. "C'mon, we better hurry or we're going to be late."

It was a short drive to the Kalet theatre and as usual, parking was a non-issue. Several years ago, the Kalet was the only theatre in town, and it was the epitome of class. Now, it was rundown and forgotten, thanks in large part to all the new cinema complexes popping up.

But to Amy, the Kalet was better than any new, high-tech cinema. Sure, it was dirty, the floor was always sticky, and she never sat on the seats without first putting down several napkins, but it was her and Brett's special place.

Thursday was horror movie night. For five dollars they could see three movies without interruption. Tonight, like most other nights, they had the entire theatre to themselves. Taking their usual seats in the back, they settled in and waited for the previews to start.

"Any idea what's on the lineup tonight?" Brett asked.

"Nope. Didn't bother to ask. Thought we could be surprised." Amy tossed some popcorn into her mouth and chewed as the lights dimmed and the credits began. The first movie up: *Scream.* "I'm impressed."

"Yeah, this isn't a half bad movie." Brett reached over and took a handful of popcorn, his fingers brushing hers as he did, sending an inexplicable shiver up her spine.

Normally, when they were alone in the theatre, they'd

talk throughout the movie, but tonight they were quiet. She wasn't sure if it was because they both actually liked the movie or because they were too preoccupied with their own thoughts.

It was going to be a long few months without Brett around. Who would she hang out with? There was her sister, Lucy, but all Lucy ever wanted to do was bitch about her boyfriend and how rotten he was. Amy had told her repeatedly to dump the jerk, but Lucy never listened.

There was Becca, the real estate agent that Amy had become close friends with. Amy could only handle that woman in small doses, though, because she was too damn happy all the time. She was one of those women who was always so chipper and tried to force everyone around her to be the same. Becca would be a good distraction on occasion, but not for a full six months, or however long Brett would be gone.

"I can't believe you're leaving me for some stupid TV show," Amy muttered.

Brett laughed. "It was your idea, remember?"

She threw popcorn at him. "Well, when have you ever known my ideas to work out?"

"It'll go by fast, don't worry." He gently nudged her with his shoulder. "Plus, I told my brother to keep an eye on you while I'm gone."

"Craig? Really?" She frowned. Craig was a good guy, and Amy liked him, but he wasn't the most reliable person in the world.

"Yes, Craig. If you need anything, you can call him."

"I know. Thanks." They fell silent again. Amy chewed on more popcorn. Maybe hanging out with Craig wouldn't be so bad. He did know how to have fun, and he always made her laugh.

"I'll miss this...hanging out with you," Brett said after several moments.

Amy smiled. "Me too."

"I might even miss you a little."

She glanced at him and saw the smile he was fighting to hide. "I might miss you, too...for a few seconds."

He laughed again. "About as much as I'll miss your stupid sayings." Brett winked.

"Yeah, well, not as much as I'll miss your lame jokes."

"Lame?" He playfully poked her in the ribs. She yelped and then laughed.

"As lame as your car."

"Oh, now that was just a low blow." He shook his head as if disgusted, but the smile that pulled at his lips told her he was faking.

Amy knew how much Brett loved his car, and her comment was said in jest, but she felt the need to apologize anyway. "Sorry. I just don't understand the whole guy car relationship thing."

"You don't have to understand it; you just have to respect it."

She laughed. "God, such a dork."

He simply shook his head, and they once again fell silent, both intent on watching the movie. Amy couldn't stop smiling. She and Brett spent a lot of time with each other, and she knew he'd miss their time together, but was it possible that he was actually going to miss her, too? He'd never said anything like that to her before.

Then again, they'd never really spent any long amount of time away from each other, either. Should she dare hope that this could be a turning point in their relationship? *Don't be stupid!* What did she expect to happen? That he'd go away for a few months and realize that he couldn't live without her, that he wanted to be more than just her friend? That was laughable.

"Did you hear a word I just said?" he asked.

"What? I'm sorry, I didn't."

He rolled his eyes. "I said don't be hooking up with my brother while I'm gone."

Amy flung her head back and laughed loudly. "Me and Craig? Now that is possibly the worst joke you've ever made." Even though she was laughing, she couldn't help but wonder what on earth possessed Brett to say that to her. Did he really think she'd hook up with his brother?

"I know my brother's track record with women. I'd hate to see you fall into his trap."

"Thanks for the vote of confidence."

"I'm just teasing."

That's what he said, but she had a feeling there was more than just humor behind his words. Tonight was their last night together, and she wasn't going to spend it arguing with him, so she let his comment go. It really was a moot point anyway, because she had no interest in Craig like that. The only Hudson man she wanted, she couldn't have.

Chapter Four

Six Months Later...

Amy hadn't seen Brett since he'd left for the show a little over six months ago. They'd talked on the phone regularly, but the show had kept him extremely busy, not leaving much time for socializing. And even though he hadn't won, he seemed to be in a great mood when he called and asked her to meet him at Gregorio's.

The last time they'd been there was the night they went to Nefarious. That had been a fun night. It was also the same night that Brett had made that ridiculous pact with her. The thought of it still made her laugh. It also kind of excited her. Would he really keep good on his promise? Marrying Brett was an exciting thought. So was having his baby.

Amy smiled and walked into the restaurant. She gave the hostess Brett's last name and was immediately escorted to his table. Her stomach fluttered at the sight of him. God, she'd missed him, missed the way they used to hang out, talk, and laugh. She couldn't wait to get back into their normal routine. Not to mention, she could really use his help at the studio. Since news spread that he was a finalist on *Dancing Duel*, enrollment at the studio had tripled. She could barely keep up with lessons.

"Amy." He smiled and greeted her with a hug.

"Hey, stranger," she said with a smile. "Wow. You look great, Brett." And he did, too. She didn't think it was possible, but it appeared as though he'd lost weight and replaced it with more muscle. It was hard enough to keep her eyes off him before. It would be impossible now.

"Here, sit." Brett pulled out a chair for her.

"Thank you." She sat and waited for Brett to do the same. "So, how are you? It's been ages since we've hung out." Amy took a sip of her water.

Brett's eyes twinkled in the way they did every time he had big news to share. "I'm getting married, Amy."

She choked on her water. Amy put her fist to her chest in an attempt to stop the coughing fit she was having. Taking another small sip, she croaked, "What?"

"Jeez, Amy, are you okay?"

"Yeah." She nodded. "Just went down wrong. Did you say you were getting married?"

"Yeah, I'm getting married," he repeated, and then smiled. "Her name is Vanessa. She's one of the costume designers for the show. I knew the moment I saw her that she was the one. I can't wait for you to meet her. You're gonna love her."

Brett...getting married? *Dear God, please let me be dreaming*. "Uh, wow, Brett, I'm not sure what to say. Would you excuse me for a moment?" Without waiting for an answer, Amy grabbed her purse and went to the restroom.

She gripped the edge of the sink and stared at her reflection.

Brett was getting married. No, this had to be some horrible nightmare. It had to be. There's no way, after only six months of knowing a woman that Brett would be getting married to her. It wasn't possible. Sure, he could be impulsive at times, but...marriage? No way.

Amy turned the faucet on and splashed cold water on her face. "Get it together," she muttered.

Taking a deep breath, she composed herself as best she could and slowly walked back out to the table. When she got there, Brett was sitting beside a thin, gorgeous, redhead. He had his arm around her shoulders, and he was nuzzling her neck. She smiled, said something, and then laughed.

Amy wanted to throw up. She cleared her throat.

"Oh, Amy," Brett looked up and smiled, "this is Vanessa. Vanessa, this is Amy."

Amy had known the moment she'd seen them at the table that the woman was Vanessa, but that still didn't stop the hurt. Brett and Amy hadn't seen each other in months, and the first time they did, he brought his fiancée here to meet Amy. Christ, a little warning would've been nice. Tears stung her eyes.

Vanessa stood and extended her hand to Amy. "It's such a pleasure to finally meet you, Amy. Brett has told me so much about you." Her voice was sickeningly sweet.

"Nice to meet you, too," Amy said her voice thick with a myriad of emotions.

"Sit," Brett said, nodding at Amy's vacant chair. "I ordered a bottle of Dom Perignon."

He bought Amy's favorite champagne to celebrate his engagement to another woman? She wanted to scream and cry. Amy clenched her hands into fists, her nails biting into her palms. Summoning all her courage, she said, "Thanks, but I have to go."

"What? You just got here," Brett said, eyeing her suspiciously. "We haven't seen in each other in months. I want you to celebrate with us."

"I know, it's just that, well, my sister called while I was in the bathroom, and I have to go. I'm sorry." Amy clutched her purse to her side and rushed out of the restaurant.

As soon as she got to her car, tears spilled down her face. Brett was getting married. Six months. He'd been gone six months, and, in that time, his entire life had changed.

She hastily wiped at her tears, got in her car, and drove home. Once there, she kicked off her shoes and grabbed a pint of mint chocolate chip ice cream from the freezer. Tearing the top open, she dug in and shoved two spoonfuls in her mouth.

"Ahh." She grabbed her forehead. Ice cream headache. "Dammit," she muttered, tossing her spoon in the sink and throwing the pint in the trash with a frustrated scream.

Amy grabbed the edge of the counter and hung her head. Her behavior tonight was rude and unacceptable. Brett was getting married – she should be happy for him, not sitting at home sulking. Honestly, what did she expect? That he would stay single for the next three years and marry her? She laughed. That was ridiculous. It was a drunken pact meant to make her feel better in the moment. It meant nothing. Deep down, she knew that.

But...she knew how things were going to go. For a while, things would be the same. She and Brett would still hang out every Thursday night like they always did; and on the weekends he would invite her to go out with him and Vanessa. Then things would change. Vanessa would get fed up with the amount of time Brett spent with Amy and demand he stop. And he would – for a few weeks or so. Eventually, Vanessa would give him an ultimatum: her or Amy. Brett would choose Amy. He always did.

Of course, he'd never been engaged before, either. And that terrified Amy. A girlfriend was one thing. A fiancée was another. There was no way Brett would choose Amy over the woman he planned to marry.

Amy drew a shaky breath as reality set in. This was it. Her friendship with Brett as she knew it was over.

She retrieved her purse from the floor where she'd tossed it and dug through it until she found her cell phone. Scrolling through her contacts, she stopped at her sister's name and hit the call button. "Lucy? It's me. I need you to come over."

"Is everything all right?" Lucy asked.

"No." Amy's lips trembled. "Please, I need you to come over right now."

"Okay, I'm on my way."

Amy wiped tears from her face only to have them replaced with fresh ones. She fast forwarded the DVD to the last dance she and Brett ever danced competitively—a sexy, sultry Rhumba. She watched the way Brett led her around the dance floor, the way he held her and looked at her.

He was so confident, cocky. And sexy. Damn was he

sexy. The way his shirt fell open, exposing his hard abs and incredible chest had distracted her so much that night. Everything about that night and that dance had enthralled her. In her mind, things had changed between them that night. Apparently, she'd been the only one who'd thought that.

"What's wrong?" Lucy said, walking through the front door. "Dammit, Amy, what's going on?" Lucy walked over, snatched the remote from Amy's hand, and shut the TV off. "Okay, what's going on?" she repeated, her tone firmer that time. "Why are you sitting there crying?"

Amy sniffled and looked up at her sister. "Sorry."

Lucy sat on the couch next to Amy. "Sorry for what?"

"I just can't believe he's getting married," Amy sobbed.

"Who's getting married?" Lucy put her arm around Amy's shoulders and hugged her.

"Brett."

"Oh...oh wow, oh my God. Brett's getting married? When did that happen?"

Amy shrugged. "He told me tonight. Apparently, he met her on the show or something. I don't know. He told me. I freaked out and came home."

"Well, who is she?"

"Her name is Vanessa. She's a costume designer on the show. She's friggin' gorgeous. She's also an obnoxious, hose-beast of a woman that is intent on destroying my friendship with Brett."

Lucy laughed. "Have you even met her?"

Amy simply sniffled and nodded. "Yeah, but I didn't stick around to get to know her."

"Maybe she's different than his other girlfriends."

With a snort, Amy said, "Yeah, right."

"Brett has never let a woman come between you two before."

She hoped her sister was right, that Brett would never let anyone come between their friendship. "I know." She released Lucy and straightened. "But he's never been engaged before either."

"You need to talk to him, Amy. Let him know you're worried about your friendship. I'm sure he'll tell you the same thing...that nothing will ever come between you two."

"I feel like the most horrible person on the face of the earth. My best friend is getting married. I should be happy for him."

Lucy shook her head. "It's hard to be happy for someone when you know they're making a mistake."

Amy stood and grabbed a tissue from the bookshelf. She blew her nose. "I just don't get it. How can he know she's the one when he's only known her six months?"

"I don't know, sweetie." Lucy got up and went into the kitchen. She busied herself with making a pitcher of margaritas. "I do know one thing, though, you have to tell him."

"Tell him what?"

"How you feel about him."

Amy rolled her eyes. "He's my best friend, Lucy."

"Yeah, your best friend who you're in love with," Lucy said.

"I'm not having this conversation with you again." Amy threw her dirty tissue in the garbage and stormed out of the room.

Amy had made the mistake of telling Lucy that Amy had always been attracted to Brett, and that she could see herself falling in love with him. Not once did Amy say she loved him. There was a big difference. But ever since she'd told her sister, Lucy had been on her case about telling Brett – something Amy vowed she would never do. Nothing would ruin their friendship quicker than professing her love for him when he clearly didn't feel the same.

And now that he was engaged, she definitely couldn't tell him. There was only one thing she could do: be the dutiful best friend and be there for him, for whatever he needed. She also had to remove herself from his life. Doing so on her terms would be easier than hearing him say they couldn't hang out or be friends any longer because Vanessa didn't like it.

"Margaritas are ready!" Lucy shouted from the other room. "Come on, sis, I know you want to get drunk with me tonight."

Amy nodded to herself. Getting drunk sounded like a pretty good idea considering how her night had turned out. She was so excited to finally see Brett and hang out with him. All he wanted to do was gloat about his fiancée. To hell with that.

"Coming," she called to her sister. "Make mine a double." She was going to need it.

"Here." Lucy handed Amy a glass. "So, what are you going to do if you're not gonna tell Brett the truth?"

Amy shrugged and took a long sip of her drink. It burned as it slid down her throat, but it tasted good. "Brett and I have talked about opening another studio in the next county over. Maybe now's the time to do that. He can continue to teach lessons here, and I'll move to the new studio." In fact, Amy had been scouting studio space while Brett was gone the past few months.

"What about all the kids here? You love teaching them," Lucy said.

"There will be other kids." Just saying that made Amy feel rotten.

She really had formed a special bond with the kids she taught. Leaving them would be hard. But staying and seeing Brett every day wasn't an option. He had a bad habit of inviting his girlfriends to watch lessons, and the last thing Amy wanted was to see Brett and Vanessa together.

"I'll figure something out," Amy said.

Chapter Five

Amy clutched her stomach and groaned. She shouldn't have had all those margaritas last night. Of course, it wasn't just the hangover that was making her sick – it was the knowledge that Brett would be arriving shortly, and she'd have to tell him what she was going to do. He probably wouldn't take it very well.

"Good morning," Brett said as he entered the studio.

As usual, he looked like he'd walked off the page of a high-end fashion magazine. Amy knew she looked like hell – hair carelessly thrown into a ponytail, face pale, skin clammy, eyes bloodshot. "Hey."

"Is everything all right with Lucy?" He dropped his bag to the floor and kicked it into the corner.

Amy clenched her teeth. "Seriously, Brett? Walk the damn bag into the office and set it down," she snapped.

"Whoa, hey, no reason to bite my head off." Brett picked up his bag and took it into the office. When he returned, he said, "Is everything okay? You seem a little agitated this morning. Is something wrong with Lucy?"

"Huh?" Oh, right, she'd lied about Lucy needing to see

her last night. "Yeah, you know her, boyfriend troubles." Amy laughed nervously. She wasn't a good liar by nature but was even worse when she tried to lie to Brett. Time to change the subject. "So, Vanessa seems nice."

"She is." He smiled broadly.

"I'm sorry I wasn't able to get to know her a little better last night," she lied.

"Well, lucky for you, we're having a small engagement party tonight. Please tell me you'll be there."

Amy felt another round of nausea threaten to send her rushing to the bathroom. She swallowed the bile rising in her throat and shook her head. "Sorry, I can't make it."

"What? Why not?" Brett put his hands on his hips and looked at her. She hated it when he looked at her like that. "C'mon, Amy, this is my engagement party. I'm getting married. You have to be there."

"I know, and I'm sorry, but I've got an appointment with the realtor to look at new studio space in Morris County. It's a prime location that's priced to sell. If I don't jump on it, we'll lose it."

"Are you serious?" Brett's eyes narrowed at her, and his jaw hung slack. "You're ditching me to go look at real estate?"

Well, when he put it like that, it sounded pretty rotten. She sighed. "It's not like you gave me much notice." Okay, that came out a lot snottier than she'd intended.

"What is up with you, Amy? You've been acting weird ever since I got back from the show."

"I've only seen you once since you've gotten back." She walked out of the practice room and into her office. Brett followed and stood in the doorway, arms crossed. "And then that was to tell me about Vanessa."

"Is that what this is about? You're upset about Vanessa?"

"No," she lied again. "I'm upset that you've been back for almost a month now and I've only seen you once. I'm upset that I thought we were going to hang out, just the two of us, only to find out you'd invited Vanessa."

Oh, crap! She shouldn't have said all that. She was walking too close to the line of telling him the truth, and if she wasn't careful, that's exactly what she would end up doing.

"You're my best friend, Amy. I thought you'd be happy for me."

"I am." She reached up and tightened her ponytail. "I guess it just took me by surprise is all."

Brett straightened and came toward her. He pulled her into a hug, which, normally, she'd openly welcome, but this time, she remained stiff. "I'll tell you what," he released her and held her out at arm's length, "instead of a traditional bachelor party, you and me will hang out. Just like we used to."

Oh, great, so now he wanted to celebrate marrying another woman by hanging out with her. Then another thought struck her. "When is the wedding?"

"This weekend. Late Sunday afternoon to be exact."

"This weekend?" Today was already Wednesday, which meant that in less than five days, Brett would be a married man. The thought had her stomach rolling again.

"Yeah." Brett nodded. "Neither of us wanted to wait. It's going to be a small ceremony just for immediate family and close friends."

"I guess," Amy bit out. She reached up and tightened her ponytail again – a nervous habit of hers. "I'm sorry. The whole thing is still a bit of a shock to me."

"No, I'm sorry. I should've told you differently, given you some more notice. So, are we on for Friday night?"

Amy smiled. She never could tell Brett no – especially when it came to spending time with him. "Yeah, of course we are."

"Great! I'll pick you up at eight. We'll go to that little taco place near your house."

"Sounds good." She nodded.

The longer he stood there talking to her, making plans to spend what would undoubtedly be their last night together, the more her heart broke. What would she do without Brett? He was the one she called on for everything. How did anyone survive losing their best friend?

"And I'll see you tonight, too, right? My mom is having it at her house."

Amy sighed. "Yeah, I'll be there." She'd rather get a root canal by a dentist with a hook for a hand than go to Brett's engagement party, but she couldn't tell him no. "What time?"

"Seven. Mom's making her homemade sauce." He licked his lips and smiled.

She tried to share his enthusiasm but couldn't even force a smile. Looked like tonight she'd have to face reality, no more running from it. At least she'd have his brother to talk to, to distract her from watching Brett fawn all over Vanessa.

That was one thing she both admired and abhorred about Brett – he wasn't afraid to show his affections in public. Amy always wanted a man to dote on her, kiss her, hold her hand, caress her lovingly without caring who was around to witness it. She wanted a man like Brett who was open with his affections. However, knowing she wasn't the object of his affections made it difficult to watch him shower others with it.

"Should I bring anything?" she asked as an afterthought.

"Just yourself." Brett grinned.

Amy arrived at Brett's parents' house a few minutes after seven. She took a deep breath, climbed the steps to the front door, and knocked. The door swung open, and she was greeted by Craig.

"Amy!" He hugged her. "Finally, someone sane."

She laughed. "What does that mean?"

He raised a brow and shook his head. "Brett has gone out of his mind marrying a woman he hardly knows."

"My thoughts exactly," she muttered, following Craig through the house and out into the backyard.

Brett's father, Dean, was manning the grill while Brett sat in a patio chair. Vanessa was on his lap. A sharp pang of jealousy shot through Amy, but she shoved it down deep. Brett wasn't hers, and he never had been. Not really.

"Look who's here," Craig announced, flinging his arm around Amy's shoulders and giving her a playful kiss on the cheek.

Brett looked up, and the smile faded from his face. He glanced back and forth between Amy and Craig, his angry gaze settling on Craig's arm, which was still around her shoulders.

"Amy, I'm glad you made it." Brett's voice was tight as he patted Vanessa on the lower back, signaling for her to get up off his lap. She did, and Brett stood.

"I told you I'd be here." Amy smiled weakly. *Just a few hours,* she told herself. Just a few hours, and then she could leave.

"Amy, dear." Mrs. Hudson walked up and hugged Amy. "Oh, it's been ages. How are you?"

"I'm fine. You?"

"Never better." She smiled. "I'm trying a new sauce recipe," she whispered conspiratorially. "I could really use your opinion."

"Lead the way," Amy said as she followed Mrs. Hudson into the house.

At this point, Amy would scrub the bathroom just so she wouldn't have to watch Brett and Vanessa together.

Chapter Six

Brett stood in the kitchen doorway watching as his mom held up a wooden spoon to Amy's mouth.

"Mmm," Amy hummed. "You've really outdone yourself this time, Ginny. This is fantastic."

His mom smiled. "You're too kind."

"Seriously, what did you do differently?"

Ginny laughed. "It's a secret." She winked.

Brett smiled. His mom had always liked Amy. He hoped that, with time, his mom would treat Vanessa the same. Clearing his throat, he stepped into the kitchen. "Dad says the grill is ready for the meat."

"Oh, okay, I'll take it out to him." Ginny pulled a tray of sausage from the refrigerator.

"No, please, let me," Amy said, reaching for the tray. "I want to help."

"Nonsense." Ginny waved her away and walked outside.

Brett continued to watch Amy, noticing how nervous she seemed. She wouldn't look at him, which was odd. Before he had a chance to question her about it, Craig came walking into the kitchen. Brett sighed with frustration.

"Did I interrupt something?" Craig asked, yanking open the refrigerator door and pulling out a bottle of beer. He twisted the top, tossed it in the trash, and took a long drink.

"No, of course not," Brett snapped.

Craig shrugged and turned his attention to Amy. "So, Amy, what do you say you and me hit the pool hall after dinner? If I remember correctly, I owe you a rematch."

Amy laughed. "Yes, you do, and this time, don't cheat."

"So, is that a yes?"

"Yeah, sure, sounds fun."

Brett clenched his teeth. He turned to his brother. "Do you mind giving us a minute?" When Craig left, Brett turned to Amy. "What's that all about?"

"What?" she asked innocently. "While you were gone, Craig and I spent some time at the pool hall. Now that I actually know how to play, he owes me a rematch." She shrugged as if it were no big deal.

"I thought I told you not to get involved with my brother while I was gone."

"You told me?" She crossed her arms over her chest and glared at him. "First of all, Brett, I'm not involved with Craig, but even if I was, what business is it of yours? You're the one getting married this weekend."

His stomach rolled at her words. What a strange reaction to the mention of his upcoming wedding. He should be happy about getting married, not feeling uneasy and dreadful. Maybe it wasn't the mention of his wedding, but rather the thought of Amy and Craig being together. Then again, he had no idea why that bothered him so much.

"I told you, my brother doesn't have a very good track record with women. He'll hurt you, Amy."

"Well, he won't be the first man to do so, and I'm sure he won't be the last."

What the hell did that mean?

"Brett?" Vanessa called, coming into the kitchen.

He smiled at her, but secretly wished she'd go away so he could talk to Amy. Jesus Christ, what the fuck was wrong with him? Vanessa was his fiancée. He should not be wishing that she would go away so he could be alone with another woman.

"Hey," he said, putting his arm around her waist.

Vanessa kissed him on the cheek. "I thought maybe you left." She giggled.

"No, of course not," he said.

"Well, I'm going to go see if Ginny needs any help," Amy said. Then she turned on her heel and left.

Fuck. Brett had no idea what just happened, but he did know that things were tense between him and Amy. Things had never been tense between them before, and he didn't like it one bit.

"C'mon," he said to Vanessa, "let's get back outside."

Brett spent the rest of the evening trying to focus on Vanessa, but all he managed to do was watch Amy and Craig flirt. God, it drove him nuts!

"It's been a lovely evening," Amy said, "but I really have to get going. As usual, Ginny, a fantastic meal."

"I'll walk you out," Brett said, not caring that Vanessa gave him a dirty look.

"That's not necessary." Craig stood. "I'll walk her out. We're going to the same place anyway."

Brett clenched his hands into fists. Of course, Craig would have to rub that in. Brett followed them to the front door. He leaned in and gave Amy a hug. "Are we still on for Friday night?" he whispered.

"Sure." Her tone was cold, clipped. She released Brett and looked at Craig. "Ready?"

"Yup."

Inhale deeply, exhale slowly. Inhale deeply, exhale slowly. Brett repeated that half a dozen times as he watched his brother leave with Amy. In that moment, he knew he'd lost Amy in more ways than one. And that hurt like hell.

Brett arrived at Amy's house exactly at eight, just like he said he would. Even though he lied to Vanessa about what he was doing tonight, he was really looking forward to spending the time with Amy. He'd missed her. He was used to seeing her more often, to talking to her every day about everything.

Knowing their relationship would change was hard to swallow. There was no way he could maintain the same close friendship with Amy while being married to Vanessa. It was simply impossible.

Sure, he and Amy would always be friends; it would just be different now. And he suspected Amy already knew that. She had to. But he was determined to stay friends with Amy – no matter what.

"Amy, I'm here," he shouted as he entered her house.

"I'm ready." She walked out of the kitchen wearing a pair of blue jeans and a long-sleeved T-shirt. Simple yet beautiful.

Her chestnut-colored hair was down, cascading around her shoulders. A touch of eye shadow accented her chocolate brown eyes and pink lip gloss made her lips look like they were sparkling. His gaze lingered on her lips a few seconds too long.

"I was thinking we could take a walk along the river and talk after we eat," she said.

Brett nodded. He had a feeling this was coming. Amy was the type of woman who liked to get things out in the open and face them head on. "Yeah, sure."

Amy smiled. "Good."

They left her house and walked down to the corner where the small taco stand was located. For being a food stand, they had surprisingly good food. Amy and Brett ordered their usual crunchy steak tacos with extra sour cream and scorching hot taco sauce. They took a seat at a two-person umbrella table and ate in silence for several moments.

The silence was mildly awkward considering he'd never felt uncomfortable around her a day in his life. He took a deep breath. "What's on your mind, Amy?"

She finished her iced tea and pushed her food away. "Are you sure you want to do this, Brett?"

"Do what?"

"Marry Vanessa. You haven't known her very long. Are you absolutely sure about this?" She folded her arms on the table and leaned forward.

He'd asked himself those very same questions not too long ago. After a moment, he nodded. "She's the one, Amy. I know it. I can't explain it, but I know." At least, that's what he kept telling himself. He wasn't sure he believed that though.

Amy gave him a sad smile. "Then I want nothing more than to see you happy."

Brett reached across the table and took her hand into his. "Thank you, that means a lot. You're my best friend. I need you by my side through this."

She pulled her hand out of his. "I would never dream of missing your wedding, Brett, but you know that..."

"Yeah, I know." He hung his head and sighed. "Things are going to change between us."

"They already have," she said quietly.

He raised his head and looked at her pointedly. "We will always be friends, Amy. *Always.*"

She had to know that. The two of them had been friends far too long to have it end just because he was getting married. There was no reason Amy couldn't be friends with both him and Vanessa. And he was making progress convincing Vanessa that Amy wasn't a threat to their marriage.

"I've decided I'm going to run the new studio in Morris County. You can continue to teach lessons at the current studio."

"What?" He must've misheard her. "We won't be teaching together?"

"I think this is for the best."

"Why?" Christ, this could not be happening. He knew things would change between them, but he did not expect this. There was no reason in hell that they couldn't continue to work together.

"We both know how this is going to go. For a while, Vanessa will be fine, and she'll even be okay with me hanging around. But then things will change. She'll get upset, and she'll want you to choose. I don't want to put you in that position, Brett, so it's better to distance ourselves now."

Unfortunately, she was right. Brett's track record when faced with having to choose between Amy and a girlfriend was consistent – he'd always chosen Amy. He knew he couldn't do that this time.

Amy stood. "I'll see you at the wedding on Sunday."

"You're leaving? I thought we were going to take a walk and talk."

"We've said everything that needs to be said." Without another word, Amy turned and left.

"Wait!" he called.

She stopped and turned back to look at him.

From where he stood, he could see her tears. He hated seeing her cry. "Please tell me the truth...are you and Craig..." He couldn't finish the thought. It was too unbearable.

"Craig and I are friends, Brett. Same as you and me." Then she turned back around and walked away.

This time, he didn't stop her.

Friends – like him and her. That was a slap in the face considering he'd never thought of Amy as just a friend. And he was pretty sure Craig didn't see her as just a friend, either. In fact, he was convinced his brother didn't know how to be just friends with women.

Brett stared after her, unable to comprehend what had just happened between them. It hurt like hell, but as she disappeared around the corner, he knew that everything she said was for his benefit. It still hurt though. A lot.

His first instinct was to chase after her, to beg her to reconsider, and tell her that nothing would change between them. No, that wasn't fair to her. He was sure all of this was just as hard on her as it was on him. Amy would see that things would be okay. Brett would show her.

With a sigh, he gathered their garbage, threw it in the trash can, and headed home. Vanessa would still be out with her friends, but that was okay. He wanted some time alone anyway.

Chapter Seven

B rett ducked before the glass vase made contact with his head. It shattered against the wall behind him. "Jesus Christ, Vanessa!"

"You spent the night with that woman?" Vanessa screamed. "How could you do this to me? To us?"

"Please, calm down."

"I will not calm down when my fiancé spent his last night as a single man with another woman." Vanessa paced around the living room.

Brett watched her closely to make sure she wasn't going to throw anything else at him. "It's not like that and you know it. I wasn't with another woman. I was with Amy."

"Amy's a woman, isn't she?" Vanessa snapped. She stopped pacing and crossed her arms over her chest. Her face was wet with tears; her cheeks were puffy and red.

"Well, yeah, but she's just Amy. She's my best friend, nothing more. You know that." He slowly approached Vanessa, hoping she'd calmed down enough to let him touch her. All the progress he thought he'd made on the Amy front was gone, just like that.

"And I told you how I felt about your friendship with her. I don't like it, Brett. I'm going to be your wife. I should be your best friend."

"I know," he whispered and pulled her into his arms.

She put her arms around him and rested her head on his chest.

He stroked her hair. "I'm sorry, Vanessa. I shouldn't have spent my bachelor party with Amy. That was inconsiderate."

Even as he said those words, he regretted them. Amy was his best friend, the one person in the world who had always been there for him. He shouldn't have to apologize for that. It wasn't fair. But he loved Vanessa, and he had asked her to be his wife. Her feelings had to come first now – no matter how much it hurt him to do so.

"All we did was eat a couple of tacos and talk. In fact, Amy and I have decided not to work together anymore." That wasn't the complete truth, but he didn't think telling Vanessa that it was all Amy's idea, and he didn't agree would only make Vanessa angrier. "She's opening a new studio and teaching there. I'll continue to teach at the old studio."

"Really?" Vanessa pulled away and looked at him.

"Yeah." He faked a smile.

It really pissed him off that Vanessa was happy about the fact that he'd given up his best friend for her. That was a huge sacrifice. Was it one he was willing to fully make for her? He was starting to question his choices as far as Vanessa was concerned.

"Thank you," she whispered. "I love you."

He responded with another smile.

"I'm telling you, man, this is a mistake," Craig said.

Brett glanced at his brother with an annoyed look. "Mom said the same thing to me earlier."

The wedding was scheduled to start in less than twenty minutes, and he was going to take his place at the altar to wait for his bride. Once he took his spot, he looked out at the seated guests.

Craig put his hand on Brett's shoulder. "We all know the woman you should be marrying is sitting out there," Craig nodded, "fourth pew back."

Brett's gaze landed on Amy, who was talking to his mom. Amy looked gorgeous as usual. She said something to his mom and then laughed. The sight of her smiling face made him smile. Until he realized that he wouldn't get to see her like that very often anymore.

"Amy and I just friends," Brett said as if on autopilot.

Craig laughed. "Stop wearing your ass as a hat and open your eyes. Amy King has never just been your friend."

"That's real nice, Craig." Brett sighed and shook his head.

Marrying Vanessa wasn't a mistake. And Amy was just his friend. He was doing the right thing by marrying Vanessa. Wasn't he?

"I'm your brother. I don't want to see you make a mistake."

"Exactly. You're my brother, which means you should

support my decision. I love Vanessa. I'm going to marry her."

Craig shrugged. "If you say so."

Brett turned and glared at him. "And you're choosing to have this conversation with me now? Ten minutes before Vanessa will be walking down that aisle. Nice timing." He went to run his hand through his hair, but stopped, not wanting to mess it up.

Vanessa hated it when his hair was all messy. She said it made him look sloppy, like he didn't care. Amy never seemed to mind though. In fact, she would laugh at him every time he messed up his hair. He sighed and turned back around to look out over the pews. His gaze once again wandered to Amy.

"It's not like you've been around much. Been kind of hard to talk to you," Craig muttered.

He was right. Brett had been very occupied with Vanessa and pulling this wedding together in such a short amount of time. "I know. Sorry."

They were silent for a few moments before Craig leaned close to Brett's ear and whispered, "It's not too late, Brett. You can still call this off."

Brett jerked his head around to stare at Craig. "Call it off? Are you crazy?"

"I'm just saying..."

Brett's heart thundered in his chest, and the tips of his ears burned hot. Breathing became difficult. Could he do that? Could he really call off the wedding? He loved Vanessa, but he didn't love her enough to give up Amy – and that's exactly what he agreed to do by marrying her. Oh, God. This was a mistake. There was no way he could marry her.

He had to stop this, now, before she started to walk

down the aisle. Unfortunately for him, the wedding march began, and he knew he was out of time.

His throat constricted as the guests rose to their feet, their faces turned toward the entrance, eagerly awaiting Vanessa's approach. He tugged at his bowtie. It suddenly felt much too tight. Plastering a fake smile on his face, he pretended to wait for his bride. In reality, he was thinking of a way out of this. He didn't want to embarrass her, but there was no way in hell he could marry her, either.

Maybe he could fake a sickness, stop the ceremony long enough to tell Vanessa that the wedding was off. Or maybe he could pretend to pass out, act like he was too weak to continue with the ceremony. No. Those were all stupid ideas. He just had to be a man and face her – tell her the wedding was off and that they were over. Brett took another deep breath and let his gaze fall on Amy. The simple sight of her calmed him, gave him the strength to do what had to be done. One thing was for certain, once he told Vanessa, he was going to...

The music stopped, but Vanessa was nowhere to be found. Brett looked around the church, and then he heard the guests murmuring, whispering, looking around. His heart felt like it stopped beating as he realized what happened. The urge to pump his fists in the air and scream with joy was all-consuming. Instead, he frowned and quickly walked down the aisle, out of the church and away from the prying eyes of his guests.

He rushed downstairs and into the basement, to the room he'd used not more than an hour ago to dress. There was a folded piece of paper taped to the outside of the door. He snatched it and unfolded it.

Brett~

I'm sorry to do this to you. You're a great guy that deserves to be happy. Unfortunately, I'm not the woman that can do that for you. It's clear to me that Amy is the most important woman in your life, and I refuse to marry a man who can't put me first.

~Vanessa

Crumpling the paper, and closing the door, he leaned his head against it and breathed a sigh of relief. *Relief!* Vanessa had jilted him at the altar. He should be pissed. Upset. But he wasn't. All he felt was relief – relief that he didn't have to marry her; relief that he didn't have to be the one to break it off; and relief that he didn't have to give up Amy.

"Brett, honey, are you in here?" His mom's soft voice carried through the closed door.

"Yeah." He opened the door and turned his back to her, not wanting her to see the lack of emotion on his face.

"Are you okay?"

He plopped down on the couch and dropped his head into his hands. "Yeah, I'm fine."

His mom sat beside him and gently rubbed his back. "What happened?"

"Vanessa left. Said she wasn't ready, that she felt we'd rushed things," he lied.

If he told his mom that Vanessa left him because of Amy, then Mom would insist that it was a sign that Brett should be with Amy. He didn't want to hear it. Not yet. He wasn't ready to face the truth.

"Oh, honey, I'm so sorry."

"I want Amy. I mean... I need to talk to Amy." Brett

slowly turned his head to look at his mother. He'd been pushing his thumbs into his closed eyes so that it would look like he was holding back tears. "Will you go get her for me?"

"Yeah, of course."

When his mother left, Brett stood and took off his jacket, draping it over the chair. Then he loosened his tie and unbuttoned the top button of his shirt. He had his back to the door, rummaging through his duffel bag when he heard Amy enter.

"Brett?" she said softly.

Slowly, he turned to face her. God, she was beautiful. He licked his lips. "She's gone," he said, his voice devoid of all emotion.

"What?" Amy walked farther into the room. "What do you mean she's gone?"

"She left." He dragged a hand through his hair and blew out a breath. "She left me a note saying she couldn't marry a man who didn't put her first." He watched the color drain from Amy's face.

"Oh, God, Brett...this is my fault? I'm so sorry."

Brett held her gaze and spoke slowly, making sure she heard and understood everything he was about to say. "No, it's not your fault, Amy. I did everything in my power to make her feel better about our relationship, to let her know that you and I were just friends." Brett shook his head.

"Still... I'm sorry."

He began to pace the room – something he only did when he was highly agitated or severely upset. Between being left at the altar and the sudden onslaught of emotions he felt toward Amy, he was ready to combust.

"I need to get out of here. I need to get out of this town. You've got your car here, right?" he asked.

"Yeah."

"Good. Get me the hell out of here."

Amy looked at him like he had four heads. "Where do you want me to take you?"

Brett shrugged. "I don't know."

He gathered his jacket and tie and shoved them into his duffel bag in the corner. Then he paused. The tickets for his honeymoon were right there, staring at him, taunting him. It was the perfect place to go, to get away from all the sympathetic looks from his family, to try to make some sense of his feelings for Amy.

"Take me to the airport," he said suddenly.

"The airport? Where are you going to go?"

He could tell by her tone that she was worried about him. "My honeymoon," he said so low she almost didn't hear him.

"Your honeymoon? What makes you think Vanessa hasn't done the same thing?" Amy paused. "Unless...you're hoping she's there so you can talk to her."

Brett shook his head. "No, she has no idea where we were going. I was going to surprise her."

"Oh, so...you're going to go on your honeymoon alone then? Is that really a good idea?"

"No." The last thing he needed right now was to be alone. He lifted the bag and pulled the strap over his shoulder. "You can go with me."

There was no better way to figure out his feelings for Amy than to spend a week alone with her, right?

"What?" Amy took several steps back, away from him. Then she laughed. "You want me to go on your honeymoon with you? No way. Uh-uh, absolutely not."

"C'mon, Amy." He gave her *that* look. The look he always gave her when he wanted something that he knew she wouldn't do. The same look that would ultimately get him what he wanted. "I need to get the hell out of here, but I don't want to be alone. I can't be. Please." Brett took a few steps toward her. "You are still my best friend, aren't you?"

"Yes, of course I am."

"Then please do this for me, Amy. There's no one else I can ask. Please." He playfully batted his eyelashes for good measure.

With a sigh, she said, "Can I at least go home and pack first?"

Brett smiled and pulled her into a hug. "Thank you, thank you, thank you." He released her. "And yes, you can pack but make it quick. I want to get as far away from here as quickly as possible."

"Okay." Amy dug her keys from her purse and followed Brett out the back door.

As they walked to her car, Brett realized it was probably a bad idea to ask Amy to go with him, but one way or the other, he had to figure out what was going on inside of him.

It was glaringly obvious to him that he couldn't maintain a relationship with a woman that wasn't Amy. So, maybe his mother and his brother were right. Maybe Amy was the woman he should be with. Lord knew he found her attractive, and that he'd fantasized about her enough. Well, it was about time he did something about it. And for all he knew, Amy didn't feel the same way, but he'd never know unless he made a move. But first, he'd spend a few days reconnecting with her, hoping he could gauge her feelings before he made an ass of himself.

Chapter Eight

"Wow!" Amy stood in the middle of the bungalow and looked around.

She was standing in the living room area, which was fully furnished with a plush, blue couch and two matching recliners. A glass coffee table was positioned in the middle of the room and smaller, round tables were scattered in between the furniture. Each smaller table held ornately decorated lamps. There was no TV, but there was a small radio mounted into the wall above the fireplace.

To her left was a small, fully equipped kitchen complete with a table and four chairs. To her left was a spiral staircase. Her gaze followed the stairs up to an open landing that appeared to be the bedroom.

"C'mon, let's go check it out," Brett said, heading for the stairs.

Amy followed him up and was shocked to find the bedroom was almost as big as the entire downstairs. There was a king-sized bed in the center of the room. She stared at it for several moments before looking at Brett.

"Um, I can sleep on the couch downstairs," she said.

"No, you take the bed. I'll sleep on the couch," he said.

"Are you sure? This is your honeymoon. You've paid for all of this." Amy glanced at the bed again. What a shame. It looked so comfortable, and she bet it felt just as good, too.

"Yeah, you're right." He laughed. "That bed is big enough for twelve people. I'm sure we can manage to share it without any issues."

Amy cleared her throat. The last thing she wanted to do was share a bed with Brett, but she didn't want to seem ungrateful, either. He had generously dragged her along on his honeymoon to the beautiful, tropical island of Tri Pinnae, which was a secluded island in the Caribbean, and it was absolutely breathtaking.

Ignoring his comment for the moment, Amy walked toward the glass double door and swung them open. She was met with a balcony that offered them not only a hot tub, but also the most gorgeous view of the ocean. The lights of the resort below lit up the otherwise dark sky.

"Wow," she said again.

Brett came up behind her. "Wow is right. The brochures didn't do this place justice," he said with a laugh.

With her hand propped on the railing, she turned to look at him. "You're in a surprisingly good mood considering."

"I'm trying not to think about it."

"Right." She nodded. "I don't know about you, but between the time difference and the jet lag, I'm exhausted." Amy yawned.

"Me too."

Amy was in that glorious state of sleep where she was half awake and half dreaming. Consciousness was slowly returning to her, but she couldn't be sure what was a dream and what was reality. So, when she felt an arm drape over her and pull her across the bed, she attributed it to a dream.

She sighed and snuggled closer to the hard, warm body behind her. The arm tightened around her, and she felt hot breath on her neck. And then she felt the unmistakable hardness of an erection pressed against her ass. Hmm... this was turning out to be one hell of a good dream.

The hand splayed against her stomach and pulled her tighter against the body. Lips brushed against her earlobe. A low "mmm" sounded behind her, and her eyes snapped open. Her heart raced and thundered so loud in her ears it was deafening.

That voice...that was...Oh, God! That was Brett's voice.

Amy jumped out of bed and gasped. Sure enough, there he lay in just a pair of boxer shorts, his erection prominent. She forced herself to tear her gaze from him, but not before she got a good look at what he was packing. Holy hell! If she thought she wanted him before, it was worse now.

"Amy...I'm...God, I'm sorry, I didn't...I was...shit," he said.

"I know. It's okay, you were probably thinking about Vanessa. You thought I was her. That's all." Amy's hands shook.

She didn't know if what she said was true, but she had to believe it. Otherwise, things were going to get super weird between her and Brett.

"Yeah. Yeah, of course. That's all it was," Brett said, nodding as he got out of bed.

Ouch! It hurt to know that while she'd been in his arms, he'd been thinking of another woman. Granted, she was the one who immediately jumped to that conclusion, but that didn't mean it still didn't hurt. No matter what happened, Amy couldn't stop hoping that someday, Brett would see her as a woman and not just his best friend.

Thankfully it was morning, and Amy didn't have to get back in bed or try to fall back asleep – both of which would be impossible.

"I'm gonna go shower," she said.

Brett watched as Amy walked into the bathroom. When she closed the door, he blew out a breath and rubbed his hands over his face. Holy shit, what the hell had just happened? Amy was right – he had been thinking about Vanessa, but he knew it wasn't Vanessa he'd reached for.

Brett hadn't expected Amy to respond like she had, which made what he did all the more awful. He was sad and lonely – and horny – and he needed someone to be close to. Amy was here. What he'd done just now, that wasn't fair to her. He knew she hadn't wanted to come here with him, but he'd guilted her into it.

Yet, he had to admit, he liked how she'd felt pressed against his body, the way she'd wiggled her ass into his erection, the sigh of pleasure that escaped her lips when he'd pulled her closer. But...did she know that it was him? Or was she dreaming of another man?

"Fuck," he muttered.

Not more than twenty-four hours ago he was jilted at the altar. The very last thing he needed was to piss off Amy and have her turn her back on him. He honestly didn't think she ever would, but he didn't want to chance it by doing stupid shit like he just did.

Several moments later, Amy emerged from the bathroom dressed in a simple blue sundress and white sandals. She looked refreshed.

"I'll take a quick shower, and then we can go get some breakfast," Brett said as he passed Amy on the way to the bathroom.

He didn't give her a chance to respond. Doing so would only lead to him saying something he probably shouldn't say. Regardless, he knew he had to apologize. Again. And he would, over breakfast.

When he came out of the bathroom, Amy was no longer in the bedroom. He went downstairs and found her in the kitchen, rummaging through the cabinets and the refrigerator. He stood and watched her for a few seconds, wondering if bringing her here was a mistake.

In his mind, his intentions were crystal clear: he wanted her. At the very least, he wanted to explore the possibility of more than just friendship. It would be difficult to broach the topic with her, though, and he'd been wracking his brain non-stop since the wedding trying to figure out a way to bring it up. Somehow, saying, "I want to fuck you, Amy, and then I want to be your boyfriend" didn't seem like a good idea.

"Finding anything good?" he asked.

"This place is fully stocked." She smiled as she turned to face him. "So, what are you thinking for breakfast?"

Brett hadn't really thought about food. In fact, he hadn't spent much time planning anything in the way of meals or activities, because it had been his plan to spend the majority of the week in bed with Vanessa.

He shrugged. "I don't know. I guess we can just start walking until we find a place."

"Sounds good. I can't wait to get out there and see the island."

He nodded and took a deep breath. "Look, Amy, I'm really sorry about this morning. I—"

"Let's just forget about it, okay?"

With a smile, Brett said, "Already done." There was no way he'd ever be able to forget how she'd felt in his arms.

"This island is a lot bigger than I thought," Amy said with a laugh.

"Yeah, no kidding." Brett wiped sweat from his brow.

They'd spent the last four hours walking the entire island, getting a feel for where things were and ideas of things they could do for the week. It was a nice walk, and all the awkwardness from earlier that morning had vanished. They were Brett and Amy again. And that felt damn good, even though he really wanted more.

"Were you serious about scuba diving?" she asked.

"You really don't want to?" He held open the door to their bungalow and motioned for her to go first. "It could be fun."

"What if we get stung by a jellyfish or something? Or we encounter a shark? I've seen that movie *Open Water*. I'm not going to get stranded in the middle of the ocean."

Brett laughed and followed her inside. "We're not going to get stranded in the ocean."

"Okay, but that doesn't mean we won't be eaten by fish."

He laughed again. "I think you're overreacting a little."

"I'm not overreacting." Amy tossed her hair over her shoulder and shot him a sideways glance. "I'm being cautious."

That look nearly killed him; it was so damn sexy. "Well, if cautious is what you're being, then we probably shouldn't go swimming right now, either."

Amy's eyes widened. "You don't think there'd be jelly-fish where we're swimming, do you?"

"Uh, you realize we're going to be swimming in the ocean, right?" He winked, knowing his response would get a rise out of her.

"That's it," she put her hands in the air, "I'm not going."

"Oh, yes you are."

"Oh, no I'm not." Amy crossed her arms over her chest and narrowed her eyes at him.

He grinned. "You are not going to spend the entire

week holed up in this bungalow. This is my honeymoon, and if I can't spend it having sex, then I'm damn well going to spend it having fun with my best friend."

Reluctantly, she smiled. "Fine. I'll go change."

Ten minutes later, they walked toward the area of the island that was designated for swimming. Brett was having a hard time keeping his eyes off Amy and his erection concealed. That thing she called a bathing suit was nothing more than a few scraps of material held together by a couple pieces of string. Don't get him wrong, she looked fantastic, but therein was the problem. He wasn't the only one noticing her. Brett frowned.

"What's wrong?" Amy asked.

"The beach is packed." He thought this island was small, allowing only a certain number of guests at a time. That was the primary reason he'd chosen to come here. "Let's go back to that place near our bungalow."

"We're not allowed to swim there. Won't we get in trouble?"

"Only if we get caught." He smiled. "Do you really want to swim there with all those people?" He nodded toward the beach.

"You're right. Okay, let's go."

As they turned to walk back the way they came, Brett wondered why he had really suggested they go somewhere else to swim. Was it truly for the reason he gave her? Or was it because he didn't want other men staring at her? Who the hell was he kidding? He wanted her all to himself. Just knowing other men were looking at her irritated the shit out of him.

"I can't get over how beautiful it is here," Amy said as they stopped at a secluded spot of beach.

She kicked off her sandals and headed toward the water. He was right behind her. The water was warm and crystal clear. He dove underwater and swam a few feet out before surfacing. Amy was still standing near the shore.

"Are you coming?" he shouted.

"Do you see any jellyfish?"

He smiled and shook his head. "No. Now get your ass in here before I have to drag you in." His cock jerked at the thought of grabbing her ass and forcing her into the water with him. He mentally groaned. *Get a grip!*

"If you're lying to me, I'm going to kill you." She slowly made her way farther into the water until it was up to her belly button, and then she went under, swimming toward him.

When she surfaced, he said, "See? No jellyfish. No sharks. Just you and me." Those words, *just you and me,* sent his stomach into a flutter. He shook it off and tried to focus on what she was saying. "What?"

"I asked if you were ready to talk about Vanessa yet. You haven't said one word about her or what happened."

"What's there to talk about? She left me." Talking about Vanessa would lead to Brett confessing the truth about how he felt about Amy, and neither of them were ready for that yet.

Amy sighed. "Okay, you're not ready. I get it." Then she smiled. "I'm here when you are."

"Thanks." He really had no idea what he'd do without her. And he couldn't believe he'd been so willing to give her up to marry a woman who obviously didn't love him. Vanessa leaving him was a blessing. "So now that you're in the ocean and haven't been eaten by fish, will you consider scuba diving?"

"Maybe, but if I do, you cannot leave my side while we're down there. I mean it, Brett." She pointed her finger at him.

He laughed. "You can tie a rope to my waist if you'd like."

"Yeah, you're laughing now, but I'm seriously going to do that."

His laughter died, and his expression turned serious. "Um, Amy," he reached for her arm, "don't move."

Her body tensed, and her eyes widened with fear. "Why?" she whispered.

"There's something behind you."

"What?" Her voice cracked, and she sounded like she was ready to cry.

He was so going to hell for this, he thought as he fought to keep his smile hidden. "I think it's a jellyfish."

Amy screamed and swam in the opposite direction. Brett clutched his stomach and laughed hysterically.

"I'm kidding," he choked out the words in between bouts of laughter. "Amy, come back!"

He swam after her, and when he caught up to her, she splashed him in the face and smacked him on the chest.

"That was *not* funny," she screamed.

Brett noticed she was shaking. "You're right, I'm sorry." He hugged her, and to his surprise, she wrapped her arms around his back and buried her face in his chest.

"I hate you," she mumbled.

Her lips tickled his chest as she spoke, and he had that same feeling from this morning – the one where his body felt like it was on fire, and he had an indescribable need to be closer to her.

He put a finger under her chin and tilted her head back so that he could look at her. His gaze lowered to her trembling lips and lingered there for far too long. What the hell was he doing?

He certainly wasn't standing there thinking about what it would feel like to kiss Amy. Just like he wasn't thinking about how great her breasts felt pressed against his chest. Or how he desperately wished she'd wrap her legs around his waist so he could sink his cock into her warm body.

"What?" she asked.

"Nothing." He shook the thoughts from his mind. "I'm sorry I scared you like that."

"Yeah, well, don't—"

"Hey! You two! You can't swim here. You swim over there," said an employee from the resort.

"Looks like we're busted," Brett said, releasing his hold on Amy. "Play dumb, it always works." They made their way out of the water and onto the beach. "Sorry, we didn't realize we couldn't swim here," Brett said to the man.

"You swim over there," the man repeated, pointing toward the opposite side of the island.

"Yes sir," Amy replied with a smile. She slipped her feet into her sandals and giggled when Brett took her arm and led her back toward their bungalow. "Play dumb? That was real smooth, Brett."

"Hey, it worked, didn't it?"

"I think the guy took pity on me because I have to put up with you."

"Put up with me? Is that what you're doing?" He grabbed her around the waist and hoisted her over his shoulder.

"Brett!" she squealed. "Put me down."

"Uh-uh. I'm going to show you what it's like to have to put up with me," he said, laughter in his voice.

"You forget I've known you a long time. I already know what it's like to put up with you."

"That's what you think." With one hand, Brett opened the door to their bungalow, carried Amy inside, up the stairs, and dropped her onto the bed. Then he proceeded to tickle her.

Chapter Nine

"Brett," she gasped. "Please...stop...I can't..." She shoved at his chest and tried to hold his hands so that he couldn't tickle her anymore. "I can't breathe."

In all the time they'd been friends, not once had he ever done anything like that. Except for when they were dancing, they were strictly hands off and in a matter of a day they'd broken that unspoken rule half a dozen times. First this morning; then in the water when he'd hugged her, and she reciprocated; then when he'd carried her back here; and now – now he was tickling her.

"Brett, I mean it!" She erupted in another fit of giggles when his fingers reached her neck. Amy grabbed at his hands and kicked her feet. "Please," she whined.

Finally, Brett stopped tickling her and collapsed on the bed beside her. They both lay there staring at the ceiling, not speaking. Amy took several deep breaths. Her mind wandered back to earlier when they were swimming. The way Brett had hugged her and then looked at her. She knew he'd been looking at her mouth. Had he thought about kissing her? Lord knew if he had, she wouldn't have stopped him.

"You're a jerk," she said once she caught her breath.

He chuckled and rolled onto his side, propping his head in his hand. "What do you want to do tonight?"

She shrugged. "I don't care. I overheard some people talking about live music and an all you can eat buffet down on the beach around sunset."

"That sounds fun. We'll go."

Amy nodded her agreement. She studied him for a moment. The look in his eyes was one she'd never seen before, and she had an overwhelming urge to pull him close, to comfort him, to kiss him.

"Are you doing okay?" she asked.

He sighed and flopped over onto his back. "I am if I don't think about it."

"You can't spend your life ignoring it, Brett."

"I know. I really just need a few more days, Amy."

"Okay." She wouldn't push him. He would talk when he was ready. "I'm going to shower and change before we go."

"I would hope you wouldn't wear that bathing suit there."

Amy picked up a pillow and threw it him. He laughed.

Amy and Brett had been at the beach party for almost

three hours, and they were having a wonderful time. Both the food and the music were incredible. They'd eaten way more than they should have; they'd laughed and danced, and they even made friends with a young couple – Jason and Emma from Texas.

"I feel like I've rambled on all night," Emma said with a giggle.

Amy smiled politely. In the twenty minutes since Emma and Jason introduced themselves, Amy knew all about them. They'd been high school sweethearts and had married right after graduation, but because Jason had been deployed to Afghanistan, they were just now getting to take their honeymoon. Jason was a Navy Corpsman – a medical doctor – and Emma was just finishing college to become a schoolteacher.

"So, tell us about y'all. How'd you meet? What do you two do?" Emma asked.

Jason kissed her on the cheek. "Don't be so nosey, darling."

Emma blushed. "Gosh, I'm so sorry."

"It's okay," Brett said. "Amy and I met when we were kids. How old were we? Twelve?" He glanced at Amy.

"Ten," Amy corrected.

"Right, well, when we were ten, we were paired together during a dance class, and the rest is history." Brett smiled.

Amy could tell that he was trying to give them enough information without giving away too much.

"So, y'all are dancers?" Emma asked.

"Yes," Amy said. "We've competed together for several years and now we run our own studio to teach ballroom dancing to kids."

"Aww, that is so sweet," Emma cooed and batted her eyelashes at her husband.

Amy noticed Brett shift uncomfortably in his chair. She turned to Emma and Jason. "It has been a pleasure meeting both of you, but I think it's time I make Brett keep his promise to take a walk with me on the beach."

She stood and waited for Brett to follow. He hadn't promised her a walk, but she hoped he would pick up on what she was trying to do – get them out of a situation that was quickly becoming uncomfortable.

Finally, Brett stood. "Yes, it's been a lot of fun." He shook Jason's hand and then escorted Amy down the beach. Once they were away from the noise of the party, he turned to her and said, "Thank you. I really didn't want to tell two complete strangers that I was left at the altar and had to beg my best friend to come here with me."

"Yeah, I kind of figured as much." Amy stopped, took off her shoes, picked them up, and carried them as she walked along the wet sand, enjoying the feel of the cool water lapping at her feet. "For the record, you didn't have to beg me. All you ever have to do is ask, Brett. You know that."

"You really mean that?"

"Of course, I would do anything for you." She didn't know why she felt the need to tell him that, but she wanted him to know for certain that she was always there for him, no matter what.

Brett reached down and intertwined their fingers, causing a devastating ripple effect on Amy's body and her emotions. He tugged on her hand and stopped her. She was afraid to face him, but knew she had to.

"Then don't leave the studio," he said.

"What?" Amy had no idea what she expected him to say, but for some reason, that wasn't it.

"I know we've talked about opening a second studio, and I think we should, but I don't want you to stop teaching with me. Think about it, we would both have to train new partners."

In that moment, a piece of Amy's heart broke. Just because being here on a beautiful, tropical island made for lovers was bringing out all these crazy feelings in her didn't mean it was having the same effect on Brett, obviously. She was a fool to think it would. No. Brett only saw her as a friend and business partner. Nothing else. Him not wanting her to leave the studio had absolutely nothing to do with him wanting her close and everything to do with not wanting the hassle of breaking in a new dance partner.

"Amy?" He tugged on her hand again.

"Yeah, okay, I'll stay," she said simply because she didn't want to have this conversation with him right now. It would ruin the entire evening.

They resumed walking, but Brett didn't release her hand like she expected. Well, she wasn't about to tell him to let go. For right now, this moment in time, she was going to enjoy walking along the beach holding Brett's hand.

"The stars are so bright," Brett said.

Amy looked up. They were bright, and they looked impossibly close, too. She'd never seen stars like that before. It was mesmerizing. From the corner of her eye, she saw Brett staring at her.

"What?" she asked, looking at him.

"Nothing." He smiled, and then added, "You just look...I mean, the way the moonlight is shining..." Brett sighed, then chuckled. "I have no idea what I'm trying to say."

Amy cocked her head to the side and gave him a quizzical look. He was acting so weird. She wondered if he'd been infested by a rare, aquatic parasite that was slowly eating at his brain, making him say and do things out of character. *Don't be ridiculous!* She really had to stop watching all those shows on Animal Planet. They walked several more feet in silence.

Then Brett said, "The way you were staring up at the stars, you looked absolutely beautiful."

"Thank you." She felt her face flush with warmth. Dear God, was she blushing?

Brett raised their hands and pressed a kiss to the back of hers. Then, without a word, he lowered them, and they continued to walk as if nothing had happened. Amy was starting to feel like she was in an episode of The Twilight Zone.

Several yards in front of them, a couple lay on the beach. The distinct sounds of moans floated on the light breeze. Amy glanced at Brett. "Are they...?"

"They're having sex," he whispered.

They stopped walking and stared at the couple with disbelief. Amy couldn't believe that anyone would have sex like that, out in the open where anyone could happen upon them. Yet, as she forced herself to look away, she couldn't help but be envious of them. That's what Amy had always wanted – a love so strong, so intense that nothing would prevent them from being together, that they couldn't keep their hands off each other.

"C'mon, let's head back." Brett turned, and Amy followed.

A few moments later, Amy asked, "Are you going to take her back? Vanessa, I mean. Are you going to try and talk to her, work things out when we get home?" Amy's heart raced as she waited for his answer. It was a question that had been bothering her since they arrived yesterday, and considering Brett hadn't talked about Vanessa at all, it was really weighing on Amy's mind.

"I'd be lying if I said I hadn't thought about talking to her," he said after a long pause.

Amy was afraid of that. Brett always blamed himself for every breakup, regardless of whether it was actually his fault or not. And he would always try to make things right, too, even if he'd been the one to end the relationship. He was too nice sometimes.

"But not at the expense of you or our friendship. I'm realizing that no woman is worth that. Besides, why rush things, right? I'm sure there is a woman out there who will love me and accept my friendship with you."

She laughed bitterly, and then clamped her lips shut. *Shit.* She hadn't meant to laugh at him like that. "I'm sorry. It's just...well, we've both been down this road before. No one seems to understand us. I'm beginning to believe that it's hopeless."

As soon as the words were out of her mouth, she regretted them. The last thing she wanted to do was be a pessimist. Brett, even though he would never openly admit it, was a romantic at heart.

"Do you really believe that?" Brett asked.

Amy shrugged. "If the past is any indication of the future, then yes, I really believe that."

"Hmm," he said like he was thinking of something else to say. "What about that one guy? He seemed okay with our friendship."

"Finn?" Amy laughed long and hard. "He was bi-sexual, remember? He wanted to invite you into bed with us."

"Oh, right, thanks for dumping that guy." Brett laughed.

Amy yawned. The bungalow came into view. She reluctantly released Brett's hand and put her shoes back on. It had been a good night.

Chapter Ten

Brett kicked the blanket off him and onto the floor; then he rolled from his side to his back with an audible sigh. When he'd agreed to sleep on the couch and let Amy have the bed, he didn't realize just how uncomfortable the couch was. That, combined with his racing thoughts, he hadn't slept a wink since turning in three hours ago.

He rubbed his hand over his chin – the same hand that had held Amy's earlier. Why he'd done that, he had no idea. But he'd liked it. His initial reaction was how perfectly her hand fit into his, which was odd considering he'd held her hand dozens of times when they'd danced. Of course, holding her hand while dancing and holding her hand just because were two completely different things.

Swinging his legs over the side of the couch, Brett stood. Sleep was elusive and continuing to lay there was only going to annoy him. Before he could think about what he was doing, he was up the stairs and standing at the foot of the bed. He watched Amy sleep, the steady rise and fall of her chest, the way her hair fell across her forehead.

Closing his eyes, he recalled how she'd looked earlier

when she stared up at the stars. The moon had cast a soft glow over her face, and he could see the stars reflected in her eyes. It was like he was seeing her for the first time, and the reaction he had to her was overwhelming. How could he have known her for so long and not noticed how beautiful she was? How smart and caring and funny she was? A part of him always knew, but he'd never really known to the level that he was now realizing.

He opened his eyes and focused his gaze on her once again before quietly opening the double doors and stepping out onto the balcony. A light breeze blew in from the ocean and caressed his bare chest. It gave him goose bumps.

He rested his forearms on the railing and leaned over, letting his head fall. Like it or not, he had to come to some sort of resolution with Vanessa. He knew he didn't love her, that he didn't want to be with her, but...there must've been something between them. If there wasn't, then why had he proposed to her in the first place?

What they shared was intense and hot. After six months of being together, that initial excitement of a new relationship hadn't faded. God, was he that desperate to settle down that he'd propose to a woman simply because the sex was good?

And Amy. God, what was he going to do about Amy? They'd been on this island for less than two days, and each moment was pure torture. Every second that passed, every smile she gave him, every laugh they shared made it harder and harder not to grab her and kiss her. He honestly didn't know how much longer he could be around her and not tell her how he really felt.

"Hey," Amy said.

Brett turned to find her standing next to him. "I'm sorry if I woke you. I didn't mean to." He was glad she was, though, because he was tired of being alone with his thoughts.

"No, I wasn't really sleeping, been tossing and turning all night."

"Me too." He resumed looking out over the balcony and at the ocean. The scent of Amy's perfume still lingered on her body and for the first time ever, he found it highly distracting. "She's tried calling a few times."

"Vanessa?"

"Yeah, I've ignored them."

"Oh."

He glanced at Amy and said the one thing that had really been bugging him the most. "I wonder if I ever really loved her or if I was just in love with the idea of her, of the life we could've had together."

Amy put her arm around his back and put her head on his shoulder. "I'm sorry."

Brett rested his head on hers and momentarily closed his eyes. This felt right. "I'm glad you're here with me, Amy."

"Like I was going to say no to a free vacation," she teased.

He gently nudged her and smiled. "Is that all I am? A free vacation?"

She lifted her head and smiled at him. "No, you're a lot more than just a free vacation."

The way she said that... the look in her eyes, the tone of her voice, it had him asking the one question he knew he shouldn't. "Haven't you ever wondered...?"

"Wondered what?"

He turned to face her. "What it would be like between you and me if we ever...?" He trailed off, unsure how, or even if he wanted to finish that thought.

"If we ever what?" Amy held his gaze, and he knew he'd have to answer her because she wouldn't give up until he did.

The words caught in his throat. If he couldn't tell her, he'd show her. He reached out and lightly brushed his knuckles down her cheek before cupping her face in his hand and leaning over. Hesitantly, he grazed his lips over hers and then parted them with his tongue. He prepared himself for the possibility that she would push him away. In fact, he was so certain that's what she would do, that he wasn't prepared when she welcomed his kiss.

Amy's eyes fluttered closed as she leaned into him and wrapped her arms around his neck. That was all the permission he needed. Brett put his arms around her back and pulled her tight against his body. He deepened the kiss and nearly lost his mind when he heard her moan.

Christ, he was kissing Amy. *Amy!* His best friend.

He thought he should feel guilty about it, that he should feel like it was wrong and inappropriate. But all he felt was her lithe body pressed against his, her lips working against his, her tongue dueling and twisting with his, and his raging desire for her. No, there was nothing wrong with what they were doing. It was good, too good. Any fears and doubts he had about it being awkward vanished the moment his lips touched hers.

"That," he said, releasing her lips, but not her. "Have you ever wondered about that?"

"Yes," she whispered, looking up at him under her thick lashes.

He raised a brow. "You have?"

Was it possible that Amy had a thing for him? Did she want more from him than just friendship? Based on the way she kissed him, he was leaning toward yes. God, how long?

How long had she wanted him? How long had he been clueless about the whole thing? If that was the case, then telling her how he felt would be so much easier.

Her soft laugh snapped him from his thoughts. "You sound surprised."

He was. It all made sense now, though. Her reaction to finding out he was getting married. Her sudden decision to leave the studio and start a new one on her own. The reality of how close he'd come to losing her rocked him to the core.

Brett lowered his lips to hers and kissed her again, this time harder, more desperate. And she responded in kind, her fingernails grazed along the nape of his neck, and then her fingers speared into his hair, holding him to her.

"Brett," she whispered.

Sweet Lord, the way she said his name had his cock thickening with need. "Amy."

"Please stop." She pushed him away. "As good as this is," she waved her hand between them, "we can't."

"Why?" He shook his head and rubbed his hands over his face. "Don't tell me you didn't feel that just now, that you didn't like it."

"No, I mean, yes, of course I liked it." She sighed and shook her head. "You said earlier that you weren't willing to be with a woman at the risk of our friendship. Well, I'm not willing to risk our friendship for sex."

Brett ran a hand through his hair and turned away from Amy. *Shit.* She was right. Sex would change things, complicate them. But God dammit he wanted her so fucking bad; he ached with need.

"I'm sorry, Brett. Please understand," she said, gently touching his shoulder.

The feel of her hand on his bare skin set him ablaze. He

turned back around and nodded. "Yeah, of course I understand. I'm sorry I started any of this. I shouldn't have—"

"No," she said quickly. "I really did like it. A lot. It was so much better than I had ever imagined, but it can't go any further."

Brett grinned. "So, what you're saying is I can keep kissing you as long as it doesn't go any further?"

She laughed. "Uh, no, that's not what I said."

He pinched her night shirt between his thumb and forefinger and tugged on it. She stepped toward him, and he took that as a sign that she wanted to kiss him as badly as he wanted to kiss her again. He lowered his mouth until it was a breath's width apart from hers.

Their gazes locked, he said, "Once more and I swear I'll leave you alone." *Yeah, right.* More like he'd leave her alone tonight.

Amy put her hand on the back of his head and pulled until his lips touched hers. Brett kissed her real slow, his tongue rolling over and around hers like a lazy river, savoring every flick of her tongue, every soft moan. No matter how much he liked the taste of her, the feel of her, this had to be it. He absolutely could *not* kiss her again or it would lead to a whole lot more – more that she wasn't willing to give. But that didn't mean he couldn't enjoy it right now. And he did. He enjoyed it so damn much that every single time she started to pull away, he'd kiss her harder. There was no way in hell he was letting her go yet.

When he finally did release her, several minutes later, he was fighting to catch his breath. He'd never kissed a woman like that before. But if he had his way, he would again. It was now his sole purpose in life to make Amy his before they left this island, before they had to return to the real world and all the distractions that came with it, because he now knew, without a doubt, that Amy was the woman he was meant to be with. He was just sorry he hadn't realized that sooner.

"Wow," she said, catching her bottom lip between her teeth.

"Tell me, do you still think being with me would be like fucking your brother?"

Amy laughed and smacked him on the chest. "Good night, Brett." Then she sauntered back inside, leaving him staring after her.

He couldn't keep the smile from his face as he walked back inside. "Good night, Amy," he said as he passed by the bed and went downstairs to the hard, uncomfortable, lonely couch. What he wouldn't give to be able to climb into bed next to her right now.

As he settled on the couch, he still couldn't believe that he'd just kissed Amy. Or that he'd liked it so damn much. And of course, now that he realized how he felt, she wasn't willing to explore it for fear of ruining their friendship, which he could understand. If for any reason things didn't work out, there was no way they could go back to where they are now. But...his gut was telling him that nothing would go wrong. They were Brett and Amy. They were two of the most compatible people in the world.

He yawned, laced his hands behind his head, and crossed his ankles. Brett wasn't a quitter. He'd figure out a way to convince her that this could work between them. He had to.

Chapter Eleven

Amy stretched and smiled. She slept so well last night. No doubt it was a result of what happened between her and Brett. She touched her lips. They still tingled from his kisses. He'd actually kissed her. How many years had she fantasized about that very thing?

And now that he'd done it, she was terrified of where it would lead. In her heart, she wanted Brett. She'd always wanted Brett. But...God, there were so many buts to consider. She knew she could not survive without Brett in her life – even if it was just his friendship – but if things didn't work out, there would be no way she could still be his friend. It would hurt too much.

But...damn it, she wanted him. She wanted him so bad it hurt. She trusted him in every other aspect of her life. Could she trust him with her heart, too? He already owned it; he just didn't know it.

With a sigh, Amy got out of bed and headed for the bathroom. Before she could grab the doorknob, the door swung open, and she came face to face with Brett. He was wet from his shower. Amy's gaze drifted down his chest and torso, lingering on his abs for a moment before lowering to the towel that hung from his hips. What were all the reasons she said they couldn't take things further last night?

"Morning," he said with a grin.

"Morning," she echoed. This is what she was afraid of – the awkwardness between them.

"I was thinking we could head over to the other side of the island and walk through the gift shops, then grab some lunch somewhere."

She gave him an odd look. "You know I'll never turn down shopping, but you hate to shop, Brett. What gives?"

He laughed. "I'm hoping if I go shopping with you, you'll go scuba diving with me."

Amy rolled her eyes. "We're back to this, are we?"

"C'mon, Amy. It will be fun, and you know I would never let anything happen to you." He took her hands and brought them to his lips, giving them a lingering kiss. "You can trust me."

"I'll think about it, okay?"

"Okay." He winked.

An hour later, Amy and Brett walked hand in hand down the stone laid pathway through the Tri Pinnae Village Shops. During their first walk around the island, she hadn't realized how many small shops there were. And there were a lot of them. There was even a fresh fruit and vegetable store at the end of the path. To her surprise, Brett followed her into every single shop and didn't complain once. *Man, he must really want to go scuba diving,* she thought.

Something in the window of a shop across the way caught her attention. She tugged Brett's hand until he followed her. Inside, she inspected the item closer. It was a necklace with what looked like a tiny seashell encased in a clear, turquoise colored rock. It was the strangest thing she'd ever seen. It was also the coolest.

"Excuse me, how much for this?" she asked the woman behind the counter.

"One hundred fifty dollars." The shock on Amy's face must've registered with the salesclerk because she quickly added, "It's the only one of its kind. It's good luck."

"We'll take it," Brett said as he reached for his wallet.

Amy jerked her head to look at him. "What? No, Brett, it's too much. I won't let you..."

But it was too late. Brett handed the woman money in exchange for the necklace.

"Thank you," Brett said to the woman, and then he escorted Amy out of the store.

"Why did you do that?" she asked him.

"Because you wanted it." He unclasped the necklace and held it out as if he were going to put it on her. "And I liked the look on your face when you saw it."

Amy lifted her hair so that Brett could fasten the necklace around her neck. She touched the charm and smiled. "Thank you."

Brett spun her around and slanted his lips over hers, taking her momentarily by surprise, but then she embraced him fully, luxuriating in the feel of his kiss. God, he was a great kisser. She could spend the rest of their time on the island standing right there kissing him, and she would be happy. It barely registered that she'd told him last night that they couldn't do this again, but her response to him clearly said the exact opposite. When he released her, she fought to get her eyes to open.

"It looks great on you," he said.

She touched the charm once again. "I love it. Thank you."

He put his arm around her shoulders, and they made their way away from the shops. Brett was acting a lot like her boyfriend today and that was a bit unsettling – especially considering she liked it so much. And it felt right, too, natural. Maybe Amy should stop overthinking this thing between them and just let her heart guide her. Let Brett take the lead and see where and how far he took things.

"Where to now?" she asked.

"It's a surprise."

His eyes twinkled in that way they always did. She loved it when he got that look in his eyes. It excited her. Amy rested her head on his shoulder, and he kissed her forehead. "And how long do I have to wait for this surprise?"

"Not long." He veered off the path and ducked under some low hanging tree branches, holding them out of the way so that she could get through them.

A short walk later, they emerged on a secluded part of the beach surrounded by large rocks. A blanket was spread out with a picnic basket on the sand beside it.

Amy took in the scene and was struck by how sweet it was of him to go to so much trouble. "When did you do all of this? How did you find this place?"

Brett laughed. "Jason and Emma told me about this place, and I enlisted Emma's help. She's a real sucker for a romantic gesture." He took her hand and led her toward the blanket. "I hope you're hungry."

"Starved."

"Good." Brett sat on the blanket and opened the picnic basket, pulling out a bottle of champagne, two glasses, and several containers of food. He poured her a glass of the bubbly liquid and handed it to her. "To new beginnings," he said.

"And lasting friendships," she added before tapping her glass to his and taking a drink. Dom Perignon, her favorite. "Is all of this part of your plan to convince me to go scuba diving with you?"

He laughed. "No. I just wanted to show you how much you mean to me, how grateful I am that you're here with me."

"Can I ask you a question without you getting mad at me?"

"Depends on the question." The corner of his mouth quirked up, and she knew he was teasing, trying to lighten the mood.

"Why now, Brett? We've been friends for years and not once have you ever shown any interest in me like you did last night. So, why now? Are you trying to use me to fill the void left by Vanessa?" She chewed nervously on her bottom lip as she waited for him to answer. Although, she wasn't sure she wanted an answer.

"I would never use you to fill a void." He settled on an elbow beside her, his hand resting on her knee. "This whole thing with Vanessa has me re-evaluating life and the choices I've made in my relationships. And I don't know...being here with you has made me see you in ways I didn't think were possible."

Her heart raced, and her breath caught in her throat. "What kind of ways?"

He trailed his finger up her leg and down again to rest on her knee. "The same way you've seen me."

She swore her heart stopped. How the hell did he know that? Amy had always been so careful to keep her true feelings hidden from him, locked away deep in her heart. She swallowed the lump that had formed in her throat.

"I meant what I said last night. This can't happen." She stood, intent on getting away from him before she changed her mind and threw herself at him.

Brett was on his feet after her. "Why not?"

"When I found out you were marrying Vanessa, I knew our friendship was over. Whether you wanted to admit it or not, it was. I resolved myself to that fact, and it hurt like hell, but I was dealing with it. And now this." She waved her hand toward the picnic and the beach. "It's too much, and I won't go through the pain of losing you again. We're friends, Brett. That's what we do best. Don't ruin it." Amy snatched her purse from the ground and walked away. Her entire body was shaking, and she hoped Brett didn't notice.

"How long?" he shouted after her.

She stopped and turned to face him. "What?"

"How long have you had feelings for me?" He walked toward her.

"Does it matter?" That was something she didn't want to tell him. It would make her look pathetic, and that's not how she wanted Brett to see her. Nor did she want any sympathetic looks or false admissions from him.

"How long, Amy?"

Fighting back tears, she looked him in the eyes and said, "Since the day I met you."

Brett didn't know what to say or do, so he let her walk away. *Since the day I met you.* Christ, how the fuck had he been so blind to that?

"Sonofabitch!" He kicked at the sand. "You just don't know when to keep your mouth shut, do you?" he muttered. "You just had to pry."

He grabbed the blanket, rolled it up, and stuffed it inside the picnic basket, all while berating himself for being so dumb._He gathered everything in his hands and went back to the bungalow only to find it empty.

"Amy?" After checking the bedroom, bathroom, and balcony, it was clear she was gone. He had to find her and make things right. He had no idea how, but he sure as shit was going to try.

All her things were still lying around, so she wasn't attempting to leave the island. That was a good sign. Maybe she went for a walk or something. He scrawled a quick note to let her know that he was out looking for her and to stay put if she came back. Then he left.

Brett checked every restaurant and shop he passed. No Amy. And no one had seen her, either. It was a goddamned island! How far could she have gone? Then he caught sight of that familiar chestnut hair coming toward him along the shoreline.

He ran to her. "Amy," he said, slightly out of breath. "I've been looking all over for you."

"I needed to clear my head. I'm sorry I ruined your surprise," she said, keeping her gaze hidden from his.

Brett put his finger under her chin and titled her head up. "I don't care about the surprise, Amy. I care about you, about us and what's happening."

"There's nothing happening." She turned her face away from him.

He clutched her chin and pressed his mouth to hers, slipping his tongue past her lips and tasting her sweet warmth. Just like every other time, she responded to him by wrapping her arms around his neck and leaning closer to him. She nipped at his bottom lip, and he groaned.

"Don't tell me there's nothing happening here," he said.

Then, without warning, it started to rain. Hard. A deluge of water poured down on them, soaking them instantly. Brett grabbed Amy's hand, and they ran toward the closest building, taking shelter under the awning. Moments later, all the lights went out on the island, casting them in near darkness. Black clouds had rolled in and stolen the sunshine.

Beside him, Amy laughed. "I say we make a run for it."

"To the bungalow? It's a ten-minute walk on a good day," he said.

"Oh, c'mon, Brett. Live a little." She let go of his hand and stepped out from under the awning. "When was the last time you played in the rain?"

He smiled and shook his head as he followed her out into the rain. It wasn't coming down as hard now as it was a few minutes ago. Amy looked like she was having fun though, so he didn't complain. She extended her arms, put her head back, and spun around, letting the rain hit her face.

Brett laughed. "You're crazy, you know that?"

"Probably." Then she took off running, and Brett chased after her.

Damn, she was fast. He attempted to catch up to her, but before he could, he lost his footing and fell flat on his back, his head hitting the wet sand with a thud. "Oof," he grunted.

Amy stopped and turned to look at him. She cupped her hands over her mouth and laughed as she walked toward him. "Oh my, God, Brett, are you okay?" She was still laughing.

Brett couldn't help but laugh, too. "This sand is a lot harder than it looks," he said, rubbing the back of his head.

She laughed harder and leaned over him. "Aww, you poor baby."

He reached up and grabbed her arm, pulling her down on top of him. Amy screamed in surprise and then started to laugh again. Brett hooked his foot around her leg and rolled her over so that she was beneath him.

"Brett!" she said, pushing at his chest. "Now I'm going to have sand in my hair."

"Aww, you poor baby." He grinned, then captured her lips in a soft kiss that quickly turned hot and desperate.

Figured she'd kiss him like that when they were lying outside in the middle of a rainstorm. He tried to deepen the kiss when he felt something cold, wet, and scratchy on his neck. Pulling away from Amy, he rubbed at the back of his neck. Sand.

"Oh, you're gonna get it now," he said, tickling her neck.

Beneath him, Amy kicked and squirmed and giggled uncontrollably. Then, before he could react, Amy grabbed a handful of sand and rubbed it in his hair. He lost focus for a moment, just long enough for her to scramble away from him.

She was on her feet in an instant. "There! Now what're you gonna do about it?"

Brett got to his feet and lunged toward her. With a squeal of laughter, Amy once again took off running. He chased her for a bit, and then stopped, gathered a handful of sand, and threw it at her. It hit the back of her leg. When she turned around and glared at him, he laughed.

"Did you just throw sand at me?" she asked.

He nodded. "You started it."

"Oh, okay." She smiled, and he noticed that rare twinkle in her eyes. It was something he'd only seen a few times, but he wished he'd get to see it more often. Amy bent and scooped up a handful of sand, which she then threw at him, hitting him in the chest.

Wow. She had good aim. "Okay, that's it," he said as he picked up more sand. "This is war now."

Amy laughed and ran away from him, but that didn't stop him from continuing to throw sand at her. His aim sucked, only hitting her once out of every five or six times he tried. He was laughing so hard his stomach hurt. As they made their way toward their bungalow, he could see people watching them from the warmth and safety of being inside, but he didn't care how ridiculous they looked because he was having too much fun.

By the time they reached their bungalow, they were both soaked to the core and covered in sand. "Okay, I give up, you win," Amy said as she approached the front porch.

Brett pulled her into his arms and kissed her. "You're covered in sand," he said, trying to brush it from her hair, which was useless because it was now mud.

"So are you." She gave him a wicked grin as she shoved two handfuls of sand down the back of his shirt.

He yelped and held out the back of his shirt in an

attempt to get the sand to fall out. A bolt of lightning lit up the sky, slicing it in half as a loud boom of thunder shook the ground.

"Looks like playtime is over," he said, ushering Amy up the steps and inside.

"I can't remember the last time I had that much fun." Amy laughed.

"Me either," he said, removing his shirt. Clumps of wet sand fell to the floor. He looked down at them and then back up at Amy, who was simply smiling at him. "Now what?"

Without a word, she reached for the hem of her shirt and lifted it off over her head. Brett's eyes widened at the sight of her standing in front of him in her bra. God, he wanted to touch her, kiss her, fuck her.

"What are you doing?" he asked when she reached for the button on her shorts.

"Well, I'm not going to walk through the place in these clothes and get mud all over everything."

"Okay, fair enough." Brett removed his shorts, too, leaving both of them in just their underwear. He slowly raked his gaze over her body before settling on her eyes. "Now what?"

"I don't know about you, but I'm going to shower." Amy spun on her heel and sauntered away from him and up the stairs.

Brett stood, watching the way her ass shook with each step she took. His hands ached to touch her, to explore every delicious inch of her body. His mouth craved to taste her, all of her. Damn he wanted to get in that shower with...wait a minute...

He took off after her, taking the steps two at a time until he reached the bathroom. "Oh, Amy!"

"Brett! Get out!" She tried to push him out of the bathroom, but he didn't budge. "You are not taking a shower with me."

"There's no power." She stared at him like he'd lost his mind. "Once you use all the hot water, that's it. There's no electricity to run the hot water heater, and I'm not taking a cold shower."

Amy laughed. "I promise not to use all the hot water. Now, go."

"Uh-uh." He shook his head. "We can leave our underwear on. It's no different than being in a bathing suit and swimming together." That was such a load of crap, and he was pretty sure she knew that, but the idea impressed him nonetheless.

She hesitated for a moment, then pointed at him. "Keep your hands to yourself, Hudson."

Brett put his hands up in a show of surrender and smiled. "I promise to only touch myself."

Amy laughed. "You're such a dork."

"Mind doing my back?" Brett handed the bar of soap to Amy. She took it and he turned his back to her so that he was facing the spray of the water.

"Who the hell knew it would be so hard to wash sand off?" she said as she rubbed the soap – and her hands – around on his back.

He drew in a deep breath through his mouth and closed his eyes. Christ, her hands felt good on his body. They were so soft and hesitant. All he wanted to do was shout his permission to the world – to let her know that she could touch him whenever, wherever, and however she wanted. This tiptoeing around, pretending like nothing was happening between them was wearing on his patience. Something was happening, and he knew she felt it.

Amy dragged her hands down his back and around to his stomach. It sent chills through his body despite the hot water of the shower. He placed his hands over hers and pulled her around so that she was in front of him. Brett took her face into his hands and kissed her. One way or another, he was going to make her realize just how serious he was about her, about the possibility of a future together that involved more than just friendship.

"My turn," he said, taking the soap from her and turning her around.

Brett lathered his hands with soap and began to wash her back. He pressed tiny kisses along the column of her neck and across her shoulders. She tasted good, her skin like silk beneath his lips. Despite washing her hair and her body, she still smelled like the beach – a scent he'd grown to love over the last couple of days.

He eased her bra strap over her shoulder and down her arm, kissing the exposed area of skin. Then he moved on to the other side, waiting for her to whisper for him to stop, but the word never came. Feeling empowered, he unhooked her bra and let it fall to the shower floor.

"Brett." Her voice trembled when she spoke.

His hands went to her breasts, which were firm and round and perky. God, she had great tits. He rolled her nipples between his fingers, and they hardened instantly. "You're so beautiful," he whispered, tugging on her earlobe.

"That feels so good." Amy tilted her head to the side, giving him greater access to her neck.

He wanted to devour her, to rip her panties off, pin her against the shower wall, and fuck her until neither of them could walk. But he wanted to savor her, too. Enjoy the feel of her in his arms, on his cock. Shit, he was so fucking hard he thought he was going to die of a stroke.

"I want you, Amy. God, I want you more than I've ever wanted anyone in my life." Brett pushed his hips into her, letting her feel just how true those words were.

She turned in his arms, put her hands on the back of his neck, and kissed him. The feel of her breasts pressed against his chest drove him insane. He eased his hands down the length of her back and grabbed her ass, yanking her tight to him. She gasped, then moaned, causing his dick to twitch with anticipation. This was it. It was finally happening. He was going to have sex with Amy. There was no going back. Not now, not ever. He had never been surer of anything in his entire life.

Brett spun her around and pinned her against the shower wall. He left her lips and trailed kisses down her throat and to her breasts. Taking one into his mouth, he swirled his tongue around her nipple, and then drew it into his mouth, sucking on it for several long moments.

"Mmm," he hummed and moved on to the other one.

Amy speared her fingers into his hair, her fingertips massaging his scalp as he moved back and forth between her breasts, sucking and teasing her nipples into tight, hard peaks.

"Brett," she whimpered. "Brett, oh God, Brett, please...Brett...stop."

And there was that one word he hadn't wanted to hear.

He put his hands on either side of her head and looked into her eyes. "Amy." He rested his forehead on hers and sighed. The last thing he wanted to do was stop. "I'm sorry. I got carried away."

He reached over and turned off the shower, which was now running cold. It was obvious she wasn't ready for this yet. But he wasn't going to give up. He'd back off, give her a little more time, and then try again.

Chapter Twelve

It had been two days. All the power on the island was still out, and it was hotter than hell in the bungalow. To make matters worse, the rain hadn't stopped, either, which meant they were stuck inside – together. Under normal circumstances that wouldn't bother him, but these weren't normal circumstances. He'd kissed Amy a few nights ago, and they'd showered together, too, but things hadn't gone any further. And he wanted them to. It was all he'd been able to think about and simply being near her was driving him insane.

"Ohh, there's a piece of cheesecake left from dinner last night," Amy said from the kitchen.

Her voice drew his attention away from the magazine he'd been holding but not reading. They'd put buckets of ice in the refrigerator to keep some things cool until the power returned.

"Wanna share it?" she asked.

Brett smiled. Cheesecake was Amy's favorite. "No, you go ahead."

"Suit yourself."

He watched as Amy got a fork and took a bite. She put it in her mouth and slowly dragged the fork back through her lips. She closed her eyes and moaned with appreciation. He felt his cock hardening as he watched her. *Fuck me,* he mentally groaned. He lifted the magazine, hoping to hell that it would distract him from her.

But then she moaned again, and he snapped. "Christ, Amy, are you eating or having an orgasm out there?"

"Sorry," she said around a mouthful of food. Swallowing, she added, "This is just so good. Are you sure you don't' want some?"

Oh, he wanted some all right – some of her. "No," he said, focusing on the magazine again.

A few minutes later, Amy walked into the living room. Brett pretended not to notice, or care, but when she was dressed like that, it was impossible not to. She was wearing a pair of really short, cotton shorts – short enough that he could see the bottom of her ass cheeks hanging out – and a very thin, spaghetti strap tank top...with no bra. It wasn't the first time he'd seen her wear something like that, but it was the first time his hands had itched to rip them off her body.

Amy plopped down on the opposite end of the couch, put her feet up on the coffee table, and picked up the book she'd been reading earlier. Brett sighed with relief. There was nothing she could do while reading that would turn him on. Or so he thought – until she tucked her bottom lip between her teeth and smiled faintly. He was instantly flooded with the memory of kissing her, of how he'd nipped at that very lip, and how she'd moaned in response.

Closing his eyes, he took a deep, calming breath – which seemed to help; until he opened his eyes and saw her rubbing her hand around her neck and throat. Then, with that same hand, she gathered her hair and held it atop her head.

His gaze went straight to her neck. The memory of kissing her there while in the shower consumed him. The way she'd responded, the taste of her, the smell of her perfume mingling with the scent of the beach – it was enough to make him want to tear the book from her hands and take her right here on the couch. By the grace of God, he was able to control himself.

But then she did something that sent him over the edge. She dragged her foot up her leg and back down again. He watched, mesmerized. She had the most stunning legs he'd ever seen, and he'd fantasized more than once about how they'd feel wrapped around him. They were his weakness. He wondered if she was doing all of this on purpose.

"Dammit, Amy." Brett stood and dropped the magazine on the table. "What with the clothes? And the hair thing...the legs...I need some damn air."

Amy lowered her book and stared at him. He didn't say anything else; he just headed for the stairs. The only place he could get air without getting soaked was the balcony off the bedroom. He felt her gaze on him as he made his way up the stairs.

He knew he'd shocked her. Hell, he'd shocked himself. It wasn't like him to have an outburst like that. Shit, he didn't even know what he'd said to her. It made no sense to him; he could only imagine how stupid it sounded to her.

Brett pushed open the balcony doors and stepped outside, inhaling deeply. There was nothing quite like the unique smell of a rainstorm. It was cleansing, which was exactly what he needed – to cleanse his mind of all the inappropriate thoughts he was having about Amy. He gripped the railing and lowered his head. What the hell was he going to do about Amy?

"Mind telling me what that was all about?" Amy said from behind him.

He didn't trust himself to look at her, so he didn't turn around, and he didn't say anything, either. She wanted an answer that he didn't have.

"Look, Brett, you asked me to come here with you because you didn't want to be alone, but it seems like right now, you can't stand to be in the same room with me."

Yup, that's what he'd told her – that he didn't want to be alone, and it was true, but the part about not wanting to be in the same room with her was all wrong. If he had his way, he'd be in the same damn bed with her.

"I'm here for you, Brett, but give me a hint, would ya? Tell me what I can do to help you. Whatever it is, whatever you need...just tell me."

"Close your eyes."

"What?"

Brett turned to face her and was momentarily awestruck by how sexy she was. It was like he was seeing her for the very first time – again. He took several steps toward her.

"Close your eyes," he repeated.

"Why? How is that going to help you?"

He smiled. "Just do it."

"I get it; you don't want to talk about Vanessa. Fine, I won't push you to talk. But this," she waved her hand in front of him, "this is just crazy. Are you sure you're not sick? Are you running a fever?"

"No, I'm not sick or feverish." He took another step closer and was now face to face with her. "Close your eyes, and I will tell you how you can help me."

With an aggravated sigh, Amy closed her eyes. Brett took a moment to let his hungry gaze wander over her body, lingering on her perky breasts, down to her flat stomach, and her long legs. He licked his lips and then lowered his head until his mouth was poised over hers.

"Keep them closed," he said.

From the way she slightly jerked back, he knew she was surprised by how close he was. "They are," she said.

Keeping his hands by his side, he moved away from her lips and to her ear. "I want you to imagine what it would feel like to have my lips kissing every inch of your body." He heard Amy's breath hitch, and he continued. "Imagine my hands tracing the path my lips had taken, exploring and caressing your soft skin."

"Brett...I..."

"Shh." He put his finger to her lips and looked at her. "Keep your eyes closed."

She made no attempt to move, other than to swallow and take a deep breath.

This time, when he spoke, he kept his gaze on her face, wanting to see her reaction. "Now I want you to imagine how it would feel to have my cock sliding into you, fucking you, making you come."

Amy sucked in a breath, and he saw the pulse in her neck quicken. His words had hit their mark.

Without missing a beat, he said, "And now imagine being trapped inside this bungalow with me, all those thoughts racing through your mind like a broken record, knowing there's not a damn thing you can do to stop them or make them go away." He paused, waiting to see if she'd say anything. When she didn't, he continued. "But that's not even the problem. Not really." Brett once again put his lips close to hers. "Open your eyes," he whispered.

She did, and then said, "If that's not the problem, then what is?"

Brett held her gaze, his mouth ready to claim hers at any second. "I don't *want* to make those thoughts go away."

"You don't?" Her voice was barely above a whisper. They were standing so close; her chest bumped his with every labored breath she took.

"No." He put his hand on her hip and pulled her tight to his body. The fact that she didn't resist or push him away was a good sign.

Amy put her hands on his biceps, her touch so soft he might have missed it if he wasn't watching every move she made. "Then what do you want?"

"You."

Chapter Thirteen

Amy's heart thundered in her chest, and it was becoming harder and harder to breathe. Her hands trembled, and she felt like she was going to throw up. Time seemed to slow to a snail's pace.

Brett wanted her.

How many times had she fantasized about hearing him say that? And now that he had, she was totally freaking out, having a full-blown panic attack.

"I need...Oh, God, room...air..." She wiggled free of his hold and walked into the bedroom, taking several gulps of air. It did nothing to calm her; it only made her dizzy. She sat on the edge of the bed and hung her head between her legs.

"Amy, are you—?"

She motioned with her hand for him to stop. "Yeah, I just need a minute to think."

"Okay."

Closing her eyes, she forced herself to calm down. Brett wanted her. It was a dream come true, but instead of embracing it, she was thinking about it. So many questions raced through her mind, but she couldn't get her mouth to form the words.

"It's nice to know the thought of being with me is so appealing," he snapped sarcastically. His voice sounded dejected, hurt, pissed off. She couldn't blame him. He'd put himself out there, and she'd basically rejected him.

Amy jerked her head up to look at him, but he was halfway down the stairs already. She chased after him. "Brett!"

"What?" He stopped and turned around, waiting for her to respond.

Slowly, one by one, she walked down the stairs until she was standing a few steps in front of him, giving her a height advantage. Drawing a nervous breath, she said, "The thought of being with you is very appealing, trust me."

Brett's blue eyes sparked with understanding, but before he could speak, she continued. "And believe me, you have no idea how hard it is to stand here, trying to do the right thing."

He took one step closer to her, and she once again found it difficult to breathe.

"And what's that?" he asked.

Amy came down another two steps so that there was no more space between them. Then she kissed him. She knew it was a mistake to do so, but she also knew that once she told him no to his little request, there would be no more kisses – ever – and she needed this final embrace like she needed her next breath.

Reluctantly, she pulled away and answered him. "Not giving into that."

His gaze bore into hers, and if it wasn't for the fact that his hands still lingered on her back, holding her, she would've run back upstairs and locked herself in the bathroom until she got her raging libido in check.

"What makes you think that's the right thing to do? Huh? Tell me, Amy, because honestly, that felt pretty damn right to me."

She pushed his hands away and took another step back up the stairs, away from him. "Our friendship comes first, Brett. It always has and it always will. I've told you, I'm not willing to risk it for sex."

A slow, cocky, self-assured smile lit up his face. "But you want to, don't you?"

"What? Risk our friendship? No." She shook her head. "Absolutely not."

His smile grew bigger, more noticeable – so did the throbbing in her clit. "No. I mean sex...with me...you want to." He took a step forward, and she took a step back. "And don't try to lie to me, Amy. I felt it in the way you just kissed me."

Damn it! She knew that was a mistake.

"You want me," one step forward for him and one back for her, "just as much as I want you."

She nervously licked her lips. "It doesn't change anything."

"So, it is true?" He took another step, but this time she didn't move.

Looking him squarely in the eyes, she said, "Will hearing me say it make you feel better? Hmm? Will it?" She didn't wait for his answer. "Yes, Brett, I want you. I want you more than you'll ever know, but that still doesn't change the fact that this is a bad idea." She put another three steps between them.

Brett seemed genuinely shocked by her admission, but he quickly recovered from it. "Says who?"

She stared at him dumbfounded. "Me. Every other person on earth who thought sleeping with their best friend was a good idea."

He nodded thoughtfully. "And enlighten me as to who said this had to be an either-or situation?"

Aw hell! How the fuck was she supposed to answer that? In her mind, it was either or because she couldn't handle being just friends with benefits. When it came to Brett Hudson, it was all or nothing. There was no way she'd survive losing his friendship if the sex didn't work out. And it would be even worse if they went from friends to dating, and then that didn't work out. No way. It was safer to just be his friend – no matter how badly she wanted him.

"One night, Amy." He closed the distance between them, and she was frozen in place. "That's all I'm asking for, just one night."

Oh, great, so he doesn't want me, he just wants sex. Tears burned her eyes.

"Tomorrow morning, we can pretend nothing ever happened if you want, and we'll chalk tonight up to two friends experimenting." He smiled. "I know you've done crazier shit than this in college."

Despite herself, she laughed. "I don't know, Brett." The indecision was apparent in her voice, and she knew he noticed.

"I've tried to ignore these thoughts, hoping they'd go away. They haven't and they won't. At least, not until I know..."

"Know what?" When he didn't answer, she asked again. "Until you know what?"

"Look, if I just wanted sex, I'm sure I could find it some-where on this island, but I don't. I want *you*, Amy."

The look in his eyes told her that he was being truthful.

But the question remained – did he simply want her for a night of consequence free sex or was there more behind his request – more that he wasn't willing to share with her?

She chewed nervously on her bottom lip. Could she do it? Could she spend a night with him, and then wake up tomorrow and act like it had never happened? Did she want to? That was her biggest fear – that this one night wouldn't be enough, that by giving in to these desires, she'd be giving her heart to him and that she'd never recover from it.

Brett placed his hand on her cheek, and she leaned into his touch. "Amy?"

Their friendship had withstood a lot. It could withstand this, too, couldn't it? God how she wanted him. She knew she'd never get another opportunity like this. If she didn't do this, she would never forgive herself. Taking a deep breath, she strengthened her resolve.

One night. That's it.

She could handle one night.

Maybe.

Chapter Fourteen

Brett swallowed hard. She was on the fence; he could tell. "The choice is yours, Amy. We can walk up those stairs to the bedroom, or we can walk down the stairs to the living room and forget we ever had this conversation." Brett searched her face, his heart racing as he waited for her to make a decision.

Ever so slowly, Amy took one step back, up the stairs. Then she took another. Brett was on her before she had the chance to take anymore. He scooped her up into his arms and crushed his mouth over hers. It was in that moment he knew – one night would never be enough. But he'd deal with that tomorrow.

Right now, he concentrated on carrying her upstairs and laying her on the bed. He brought his body over hers, kissing her, letting his hand roam down the length of her body. It was so tempting to tear the clothes from her body and ravage her.

"Brett," she whispered, turning away from his kiss.

He groaned. "Amy, baby, please don't stop me. Not now."

He knew clear to his soul that if they didn't take this plunge, he'd never be able to see her with another man. It would kill him. Or rather, he'd kill the other guy for touching what belonged to him.

Brett gently took her chin in his thumb and forefinger and turned her to look at him. He brushed his lips over hers. "I want you so much, Amy."

"I want you, too."

"Then what's the problem?"

"Nothing...I..." Amy grabbed his face and kissed him hard.

He gathered both of her hands into his and pinned them above her head, lacing their fingers together as she spread her legs, and he settled between them. "Keep your hands there," he said.

Then he kissed her chin, down her throat, stopping once he reached the material of her shirt. Sliding his hands up into her tank top, he pulled it off over her head. His gaze lingered on her breasts and her hard nipples. His cock was so hard he thought he was going to die.

"You're so beautiful," he breathed out.

Brett found her mouth again and kissed her deeply as he leisurely ran his hand down her arm, along her breast and to her waist, memorizing every soft curve of her body.

"You're trembling," he said.

"I'm scared."

"Why?" He flexed his fingers on her waist in an attempt to reassure her that it was okay, that he wouldn't do anything she didn't want him to, and that she could set the pace.

"Because it's you."

Brett smiled. "That sounds like a reason why you shouldn't be scared."

"Yeah, well, I think it's having the opposite effect on me. What if—"

He put his finger to her lips to silence her. "Don't."

He knew what she was going to say. What if it's not good? What if we're not sexually compatible? What if, after we do it, we decide we didn't like it? Or something along those lines. He wouldn't let those thoughts, those doubts and fears ruin this moment for them.

"Just relax, okay?" Brett winked, kissed her softly on the lips, and then moved down her body.

Brett stopped at her breasts, taking one into his mouth and the other into his hand. The feel of her hard nipple rubbing against his tongue and hardening between his fingers had his cock thickening with need. *Slow down.* He would not rush this. Oh no, he was going to take his time and explore every inch of her body until it was permanently ingrained in his mind and on his tongue.

Amy arched her back and speared her fingers into his hair. "Yeah," she whispered and dragged his face up to hers.

He obliged and gave her exactly what she wanted – a kiss that was so hot and deep and passionate she ground her sex against his leg. Brett smiled against her lips and put his hand on her waist, pinning her to the bed.

"You're making it very hard to take this slow," he said.

"Going slow is overrated." Amy pushed him off her and rolled on top of him.

The action took him by surprise, but he liked her aggressiveness and decided to go with it for the moment. "Now what are you going to do?"

She gave him another wicked smile. "This." She pressed her lips to his chest, her tongue licking across his pecs and to his nipple.

He put one hand behind his head and used the other to

hold her hair away from her face so that he could watch her, a deep, throaty groan escaping from him.

"And this." Amy kissed down his torso to his belly button, swirling her tongue in his navel. It felt weird in an erotic sort of way.

"Oh, and this," she said, curling her fingers into the waistband of his shorts and tugging them down over his hips, allowing his cock to spring free in all its hard glory. She looked up at him under her lashes, and then wrapped her hand around his shaft, squeezing just enough to cause his hips to jerk up off the bed. Then she licked the ridge of his cockhead, drawing him deep into the back of her throat.

"Fuck," he groaned. Sonofabitch her mouth was so hot and wet and... Christ, she was deep throating him! He sucked in a breath, his stomach hollowed, and his mouth was stuck in the shape of an O as he fought not to blow his wad already. What the hell? He wasn't a horny, sex-starved teenager. Nor was this his first blow job. So why in the hell was he fighting to hold back his release so soon?

"Mmm." She sucked on his head while stroking his shaft with her hand.

Her moans reverberated down his shaft and landed in his balls like a sack of bricks. That familiar tingling at the base of his spine started to spread through his body, and he knew he was going to lose it if he didn't stop her.

"Amy." He gathered her hair into his hands and was mesmerized by the sight of her pretty, pink lips wrapped around his cock. It was something he never thought he'd see, which only added to the intensity of it. "Holy shit that feels good."

"Tastes good, too." She looked at him, smiled, and licked her lips.

"Okay, that's it." Brett reached for her, flipped her over

onto her back, and pinned her beneath his body. He found her lips and parted them with his tongue. Pouring everything he felt for her into that kiss, he left her wanting more as he slid down her body. "Now it's my turn." Brett removed her shorts and was shocked to find her shaved. He jerked his gaze up to hers and grinned.

"What?" she asked self-consciously.

Brett shook his head. "Nothing...it's just...you're full of surprises."

"Is that a bad thing?"

"You tell me." He sat on his knees, took her hand, and put it on his cock. "Feel how hard you've made me?" She nodded and started to stroke him again. He felt his knees buckle as he leaned over to kiss her again. "I think it's safe to say I like your surprises."

Amy smiled. "Good."

He lowered his body, and then his head between her legs and firmly kissed her mound before parting her folds. Licking up one side, and then down the other, he closed his eyes and savored the intoxicating sweetness of her.

Amy moaned when he sucked her clit into his mouth, then released it only to suck on it once again. No woman had ever tasted as good as she did, and he knew that he'd made the right decision to cross this line with her. With each flick of his tongue over her pussy, he was branding her, marking her as his. And each time she cried his name and moaned with pleasure, she solidified her place in his heart and body.

Amy bucked beneath him, her hips lifting to meet his mouth as she clutched at his hair. "Oh God, Brett, yes..."

He eased two fingers inside of her while continuing to tease her clit with his tongue. "You taste so good, so good."

She tightened around his fingers, and he knew she was

close to coming. God, he wanted to taste her release on his tongue and on his hand and on his cock. Fucking Christ, he wanted all of her everywhere at once. Brett slipped another finger into her and pressed his thumb to her clit; then he moved up to her mouth, claiming her lips in a kiss.

Her fingernails dug into the hard flesh of his biceps, and her thighs clamped around his arm, making it difficult to move his fingers inside of her, but he persisted.

"Brett," she whimpered into his mouth.

"That's right. Come for me, baby." He nipped at her bottom lip and curled his fingers against her inner walls, stroking them to their breaking point.

Moments later, she came apart in his arms, crying his name as she came. It was the single most erotic thing in the world to hold her in his arms as she showered his hand with her release.

"Oh...my...God," she panted.

Brett eased his fingers from her, anxious to replace them with his cock, which was ready to burst if he didn't bury it inside of her soon. But first, he needed to get a condom. He'd packed several boxes that he'd never bothered to remove from his suitcase before leaving. Thank heavens for that.

Before he could retrieve one, Amy clutched his face and kissed him. "I need you, Brett. I need to feel you inside of me. Now, please."

Her low, raspy, pleading voice was his undoing. "Condom," was all he said even though he was already settling between her spread legs, knowing full well that he would never make it across the room to get one.

"I'm on the pill." She wiggled her hips beneath him, tempting him, enticing him to take her just like they were.

"Aren't you worried about diseases?" *Smooth one,*

Hudson; that was real romantic. He positioned the head of his cock at the clenched opening of her pussy.

"Why? Do you have one I should know about?"

He laughed. "No."

"Well, neither do I. Now, stop teasing me." She wiggled again.

Teasing her? Oh, he would show her just exactly how serious he was about *not* teasing her. He slowly pushed inside of her, and they moaned simultaneously. She was much tighter than he'd expected, and her pussy enveloped his cock like a glove, snug and warm.

Brett was a hard ass when it came to safe sex, and this was the first time he'd ever had sex without a condom. Seemed rather poetic that it was with Amy. It was fantastic, and he knew that he'd never again wear a condom. Not as long as he was with Amy, which, if he had his way, would be forever.

The sensations of her wet pussy gripping his cock each time he'd thrust in and out of her was like billions of fireworks going off in his mind and body. He was on an overload of pleasure that he didn't want to end. The world could end in a fiery blaze, and he wouldn't notice.

She reached around and grabbed his ass, holding him deep inside of her as she rotated her hips, grinding her pussy on him. "God, Brett...ahh," she yelled.

"Christ you feel so good, Amy, so fucking good...I can't..." He stilled inside of her, knowing that one slight move would have him coming instantly, and he wasn't ready for that yet.

Brett smoothed the hair from her forehead and gave her a soft, languid kiss. She scraped her fingernails up the length of his back, making him shudder. Then, with agonizingly slow movements, he began to move in and out of her again.

He was doing good keeping his pace steady, letting the pleasure build between them until they were both ready to explode, but when she raked her teeth along his neck, he lost it. Thankfully, she was on the precipice, too, because there was no stopping it this time.

"Brett!" His name fell from her lips as a chant.

"Fuck, Amy." He shifted his weight into his arms and fucked her with jackhammer quick thrusts until they both gave in to their orgasms.

She clenched his dick so hard it was almost painful, but nothing could've prepared him for what it would feel like to have her hot come cover his bare cock as he spilled into her. Coming inside of a woman, this woman, his woman – Amy – without the barrier of a condom was the best feeling ever. He swore he momentarily blacked out from the pleasure of it, of her.

Brett buried his face in her neck and tried to calm his breathing. He felt her heart beating just as hard as his when he kissed her neck and throat. "You okay?" He dragged his mouth to hers and kissed her.

"Never better." She smiled.

Outside, the rain continued to come down in sheets. Thunder shook the earth around them, and the consistent bolts of lightning were the only illumination in the now dark bungalow. None of it made any difference to Brett because all his attention was focused on Amy and the feelings that he had for her. There was only one thing on his mind: forever.

Chapter Fifteen

Amy awoke early the next morning, wanting to get out of bed and dressed before Brett woke up. She allowed herself a moment to admire his naked body, though. He was gorgeous, sexy, and holy hell did he know what he was doing in the bedroom.

She closed her eyes and let the memory of last night fill her mind. Her fantasies did *not* do that man justice. Holy crap, he was fantastic. And big! Good God, he had the biggest cock she'd ever seen. But...their one night was over and all she had now were her memories of the best sex of her life. With a sad sigh, she gently tried to ease out of bed.

Before she could get too far, Brett reached out and grabbed her around the waist. In one swift movement, he pulled her to him, rolled her onto her back, spread her legs with his knees, and pushed into her. Then he just stopped.

"Brett, what are you doing?" she gasped with surprise...and pleasure.

Without a word, he rolled them over so that she was now on top of him. Instinctively, she brought her knees up to rest on either side of his waist and straddled him. He put his hand on the back of her head and brought her down to his lips, kissing her slowly. She moaned into his mouth, the desire to move on him, to ride him was overwhelming.

"Brett, no, we agreed. One night, remember?" She looked down at him but made no effort to move.

"One night wasn't enough, Amy. I want more." His voice was deep, heavy with sleep, and sexy as hell. He ran his hands down her back and gripped her ass, squeezing her cheeks, and then pushed her down on his cock as he lifted his hips to meet her.

"Oh, God," she moaned. Christ, how was she supposed to think when he was buried inside of her?

"The choice is yours again," he said, kneading her ass in his hands. "You can get up and we'll move on like last night never happened, or we can do this again." He rotated his hips ever so slightly, just enough so that she felt the movement.

"Brett." She tried to sound serious, but it came out as needy.

Amy put her hands on either side of his head and stared at him. His eyes weren't the normal crisp blue that she was used to seeing. No, they were hazy and filled with desire. How much more did he want? Once? Another full night? It was one of those questions that she wasn't sure she really wanted an answer to. So, she did the only thing she could – she eased her body up and off him.

Brett grabbed her waist. "Amy, please," he pleaded.

She smiled as she lowered herself back down onto him. And that's all it took. Amy found his lips and kissed him hard as she rotated her hips on him, driving his cock deeper into her with each downward motion of her body.

"God, Brett," she groaned, "nothing should feel this good."

"You do." He nipped at her bottom lip. Digging his heels into the mattress, he tightened his grip on her ass and fucked her hard and fast.

She met each of his upward thrusts with a downward one of her own. The sounds of their moans reverberated around them. It was hard to believe, but she was so close to coming already. The way he moved in and out of her, the way he held her, kissed her, moaned in between their kisses was incredible. Hell, everything about Brett Hudson was incredible.

And she was hopelessly in love with him. She'd loved him before they'd had sex. It was worse now. Her feelings wouldn't be so easy to hide anymore. She wasn't sure she wanted to. There was one thing she was sure of, though – she'd give herself to him for as long as he wanted. That probably made her sound pathetic, but at the moment, all she cared about was being with him.

Brett moved one hand back up to palm her head, the other remained on her ass, guiding her up and down on his cock. "Fuck, Amy, you feel incredible." He kissed her, his tongue invading her mouth with a frantic, needy, desperation that she matched stroke for stroke.

"Yeah," she moaned, increasing the speed at which she moved on him. She curled her fingers against his chest, her nails digging into his skin as sat up fully on him. "So good."

She flung her head back and closed her eyes. The feel of straddling Brett, of his cock stroking her inner walls, driving her to madness was euphoric. Amy never thought sex could be so good, so fulfilling while still making her crave more.

His large, warm hands covered her breasts, his thumbs rolled over her nipples, sending an extra jolt of pleasure straight to her clit. "God, I can't get enough of you, Amy."

He clutched her hips and then sat up so that they were chest to chest.

She hooked her legs around his back and rocked on him as their mouths explored each other like it was the first time they'd ever kissed.

Amy leaned back and guided Brett's mouth to her breast. She gasped and then moaned when he tugged her nipple between his teeth. The things this man could do with his tongue and mouth should be illegal it was so damn good. The tip of his tongue circled her hard nipple, making it even harder. Then he blew on it, causing her to tremble in his arms. Dear God, she was ready to explode from the feelings he brought out in her.

Brett slid his hands from her lower back up to her shoulder blades, bringing her to an upright position again, and finding her lips. Instead of kissing her, he traced her lips with his tongue, then nipped at them. The fact that it was still dark in the room, and she couldn't see a thing, made everything he did that much more exciting.

"Kiss me," she demanded.

He did, and the world exploded around her. The room began to spin; her mind went fuzzy; and the only thing she could focus on was Brett's cock inside of her, of her pussy clenching, desperate to hold him there as her clit throbbed with her impending release. She rocked on him harder and faster, her moans getting louder as he swelled inside of her.

"Come for me, baby," he whispered, nipping at her ear.

In all the time she'd known Brett, she'd never once heard him call a girl baby or any other term of endearment like that. Of course, she didn't know what happened when he was in bed with those other women, and she didn't want to. For the time being, she wanted to believe that she was special, that this was a first for him.

"Amy," he groaned, "please, baby, I want to feel you come on my cock again."

She loved when he talked like that, and when he called her baby. They both increased the speed and intensity of their movements until she screamed his name and dropped her forehead to his shoulder. That one orgasm was more intense than the two she'd had last night. How was that possible? Oh, who cared! As long as he continued to make love to her like that, he could do whatever the hell he wanted to her and her body.

If she wasn't a hundred percent sure before – and she was – there were no doubts now. Amy was head over heels in love with Brett Hudson, the kind of love that would destroy her if not reciprocated by him. She just hoped to hell that Brett felt the same.

It took several moments for the tremors to ease from her body, leaving her limp and spent. Brett showered her shoulder and collarbone with kisses. She stroked the nape of his neck, holding on to him for as long as she could.

"I don't think I'll ever get enough of this, of you," he said in between kisses.

"Mmm," she said sleepily. "Me either." They sat like that, in each other's arms for several more minutes before Amy finally pulled away. "I'm starving."

Brett laughed. "Me too."

Reluctantly, Amy got off his lap and out of bed. She searched for her cell phone and turned it on, using the screen as a flashlight to help find her clothes.

Brett did the same, and as soon as he was dressed, he went downstairs to find and light some candles. When she was sure he was out of sight, she did a little happy dance and squealed with excitement.

She and Brett were together! For a little while, anyway. It was a dream come true. Finding a clean pair of black silk panties and a matching silk tank top, she put them on and went downstairs to help Brett.

He'd found an entire cabinet full of candles and had lit half of them by the time she made it to the kitchen where he had the unlit ones spread across the table. The living room and part of the kitchen was aglow in candlelight. It would be romantic if it wasn't necessary.

Brett stopped with the lighter halfway to the wick of the candle he was holding. "What're you wearing?"

Amy smiled. "What?" she asked innocently. "There's no power, the air doesn't work, and it's hot in here."

He devoured her with his eyes for a moment before finally speaking again. "You're wearing fuck me clothes," he said as he turned his attention back to lighting the candles.

"So what if I am? What're you going to do about it?" She crossed her arms over her chest.

"I'm going to fuck you." He lit another candle. "Repeatedly."

Amy's breath caught in her throat. His words dripped with promise, and the way he said that, so calm and self-assured, had her squeezing her thighs together to stop the throbbing in her clit. She swallowed hard when Brett put the lighter down and came toward her.

He trailed his hand over her ass cheek and down her thigh, giving it a firm squeeze. "You're lucky I don't rip this off you, bend you over this table, and take you right now." His voice was deeply sexual, husky.

Her heart took off like a runaway freight train, pounding in her chest so hard she thought she would break a rib. "That could be fun," she said.

"Better yet," Brett lifted her up, set her on the counter, and stood between her legs, "maybe I'll just tease you until you beg for my cock." He pressed his thumb to her panties and circled her clit.

Amy sucked in a breath and opened her legs a little wider, loving the way he touched her, stroking her desire to an out-of-control level. Then again, simply being around him had that effect on her. He didn't have to tease her to get her to beg. She was willing to do that at any given time.

She groaned when Brett stopped touching her. "Two can play this game, y'know?"

He put his hands on the counter on either side of her legs, put his face inches from hers, and said, "Let the games begin."

Brett's ringing cell phone prevented Amy from responding. He pulled it from his back pocket, looked at the screen, smiled, and then answered. "Hello?"

"Are you dead in a ditch somewhere or did you forget how to use that fancy cell phone of yours?"

Brett's mom. From the tone and level of her voice, Amy knew Ginny wasn't happy with Brett. Amy smiled. Mrs. Hudson was funny when she got angry with Brett. She was also feisty as hell.

"No, Mom, I'm fine." He put the call on speaker and held the phone away from his ear. "There's no need to yell."

"Brett Matthew Hudson! Do not tell your mother not to yell when you promised to call and haven't. One minute you're in the basement of the church and the next you're on a plane flying across the country with no warning at all. And before you say anything, leaving a message on our answering machine is not acceptable. What the heck is wrong with you? Why on earth would you go on your honeymoon alone? You should be with people who care about you, who can help you through this."

"I'm sorry," he said, fighting to suppress a smile.

Amy eyed him curiously. What was he up to?

"I should've let you know that I was leaving, and I should've called to let you know I was okay," he said.

Amy leaned forward and kissed him on the cheek. He wasn't a momma's boy, but he did love and respect his mother – a quality Amy always admired and loved.

"Damn right you should have." Ginny sighed. "So, how are you? Are you doing okay? You're eating and taking care of yourself right?"

"Yes, Mom." Brett rolled his eyes.

Amy smacked him on the chest and mouthed the words, "Be nice."

"I'm fine, I promise. I'm eating and relaxing and taking care of myself," he said.

"Are you sleeping?" Ginny pressed.

Brett looked at Amy and winked. "Not as much as I should be."

Amy felt her face flush with warmth. She hoped to God Brett didn't tell his mother about them. Not yet anyway. Amy was still adjusting to the idea, and she wanted to keep Brett – and their new relationship – all to herself for a little bit longer.

"You shouldn't be alone, Brett. Please, come home. You can stay with me and your father for a few days. Your brother is still here, too."

"Mom." He laughed. "I'm not alone."

"You're not? Well...who're you with?" Ginny paused for a brief moment, and then added, "Oh, Brett, please don't tell me you met someone."

He laughed again. "Relax, Mom, I'm here with Amy."

"Amy? What...how...? You put her on the phone right now."

"Okay, hold on." Brett turned the speaker off and held the phone behind his back.

Then he captured Amy's lips in a kiss that took her momentarily by surprise. She closed her eyes and leaned into him, savoring the taste of his tongue probing her mouth, of his soft lips working against hers.

He broke the kiss and whispered, "Don't tell her about us, okay?"

"Yeah, okay." She knew why she didn't want to tell Ginny, but why didn't Brett want her to know? He handed her the phone and she took it. "Hello, Mrs. Hudson." Amy hopped down off the counter and walked into the living room.

"Oh, Amy, dear, I'm so glad to hear you're with Brett. Tell me, how's he doing? Honestly."

Amy turned to look at Brett, who was leaning against the counter and smiling at her. "He's doing just fine, Mrs. Hudson, I promise. I'm taking good care of him."

"You have no idea how happy I am to hear that. Whatever you do, do not let him go back to that horrid woman."

Amy laughed. "I don't think that's going to be a problem."

"Good. When you get back, Dean and I want to have you over for dinner."

"Sounds like a plan." She glanced at Brett. He had a look on his face that said, "What are you getting me into?" Amy waved her fingers at him and then turned her back on him.

"Okay, you two take care and have fun. Be sure my son calls me tomorrow."

"I will." Amy hung up, then handed the phone back to Brett.

"So? What did she say?"

"That I was to take care of you, make sure you don't go back to that horrid woman, and that I had to come over for dinner when we got back."

Brett laughed. He took the phone from her hand and pulled her into his arms. "I have to agree with my mom's orders this time."

"Oh yeah?"

"Yeah." He closed the short distance between them and slanted his lips over hers, kissing her with a soft determination. "At least I don't have to worry about my parents liking you."

Amy laughed. "You really are such a dork."

"Okay, well this dork is going to go get us some food. What do you want?"

"Surprise me."

He winked. "You got it."

He headed toward the door and then stopped. Turning around and walking back to her, he slid his hand over her cheek and into her hair.

Brett kissed the top of her head and said, "I'm so sorry, Amy."

She turned her face up to look at him. "For what?"

"For not seeing what's been right in front of me all this time."

"Don't be sorry. You had no idea how I felt about you," she whispered.

He put his hands on either side of her face and stroked her cheeks with his thumbs. "You're my best friend. I should've known."

She pressed her lips to his and answered him with a

kiss. He wrapped his arms around her back and held her tight to his body. Kissing him, being in his arms would never get old. Amy was exactly where she always wanted to be, and she would do whatever it took to keep things just as they were right then.

Chapter Sixteen

"I can't possibly eat another bite," Amy said.

Brett knew bringing back Italian food – chicken Parmesan, which was Amy's favorite was a safe bet. He was glad he'd suggested piling pillows and blankets on the living room floor and eating there as opposed to at the table. It was cozier, more intimate.

Brett held out his fork with a piece of chicken on it. He leaned forward. "You know you want another taste."

Amy looked back and forth from him to the food. He nudged the food closer to her lips, but when she went to take it, he pulled it away and kissed her instead.

"Mmm," she said, licking her lips.

"You taste so much better than this food," he whispered as he leaned over to kiss her again.

"I was just thinking the same thing." She smiled against his lips.

God, he wanted to lay her down on the floor and have his way with her. He wanted to kiss and lick his way down her body; he wanted to taste her pussy on his tongue; he wanted to feel her wrapped around his cock as he fucked her into orgasm after orgasm. But he didn't get a chance to do any of that because there was a knock on the door.

"Are you expecting company?" she asked him, her tone teasing.

"No, but you stay put." He pointed at her, then stood. There was no way he would let her answer the door when she was still only dressed in those panties and tank top. Brett went to the door and opened it.

"Mr. Hudson?"

"Yes."

"I'm George Rinaldo from Tri Pinnae Resort Hospitality. I'm just taking a moment to see how you're doing. The island is still without power, but we've been assured we'll have it back tomorrow morning. In the meantime, the hotel is operating on a generator. Hot food and showers are available there for all guests."

"Thank you, Mr. Rinaldo," Brett said.

"Anytime, sir. Is there anything you need?"

Brett looked over his shoulder into the bungalow. "No, I don't believe so."

"Oh, one more thing, for safety reasons, we're asking that guests don't wander the island until the power is restored. There are broken tree branches and other debris," George said.

"No problem." Brett smiled. "Have a nice evening." He closed the door and turned to Amy. "Looks like you and I are stuck in this bungalow together for the rest of the night." And he had plenty of ideas about what they could do to pass the time.

"I don't see a problem with that at all," she said.

"Good." He winked.

Together they cleaned up the remnants of their dinner. Amy took care of the trash while Brett opened the wine he'd bought earlier. Getting two glasses, he filled them and carried them back into the living room. He sat on the floor with his back against the couch. Amy sat next to him.

Handing her a glass of wine, he said, "To us."

"Us," she agreed with a smile.

They sat and silently sipped their wine. Outside, it began to rain again. Thunder boomed and bolts of lightning lit up the dark night sky. He took their glasses and set them on the end table. Amy rested her head on the couch, closed her eyes, and sighed. Brett watched her with a faint smile on his lips.

She was so beautiful. The way her chestnut hair fell around her face, framing it like a priceless piece of art, stole his breath. He trailed the back of his hand down the side of her face and tucked her hair behind her ear. She opened her eyes and looked at him. His heart swelled and then constricted.

"Amy," he whispered, his voice wavering slightly. There was so much he wanted to say to her, but he had no idea where to begin.

She reached up and touched his face, her hand trembled. "I still can't believe this is actually happening between us."

He lowered his lips to hers so that they brushed when he spoke. "Believe it." He nipped at her bottom lip and then kissed her. Slow at first, then deeper, harder. Brett pulled her onto his lap, and she straddled him. He had an overwhelming desire to please her. "Tell me what you want, baby."

"I want you." Her voice was a breathless whisper.

"You have me." He slipped his hands up the back of her tank top and slid it up over her head. He tossed it to the floor and settled his hands on her waist. "Tell me what else you want."

"I want you to touch me." Amy took his hand, placed it on her stomach, and then pushed it down into her panties.

"Like this?" Brett slid his finger between her damp folds, dragging it up and down a few times before settling on her clit, rubbing it with a firm gentleness.

Amy inhaled sharply, and her head fell back to her shoulders. "Yeah, just like that."

Brett's gaze was focused intently on her. She began to move her hips in a circular motion, matching the rhythm of his finger. "What else?"

"Oh, God," she moaned.

He stilled his finger. "Tell me what else you want, Amy."

She grabbed his hand and ground her pussy against it. "I want you to keep doing that."

"And?"

Taking his other hand, she put it on her breast. He kneaded it and rolled her nipple between his thumb and forefinger, causing it to harden in his grip.

She gripped the back of his head and brought his mouth to her nipple. "Lick it," she ordered.

Smiling, he closed his mouth around her hard nipple. He flicked his tongue over it, nipped at it, and then sucked on it again. Amy arched into him and moaned. Christ, the sounds of her moans drove him wild.

"Mmm." He planted a kiss to her nipple, then moved on to the other one.

Amy grabbed a handful of his hair and yanked his head back, crushing her mouth to his. Her hips rotated faster, harder. "I'm gonna come," she whimpered into his mouth.

Brett eased his finger from her clit, down her folds, and

into her pussy. She dug her fingernails into his shoulders and cried his name.

"Yeah, that's it, baby, come for me." He caught her bottom lip between his teeth as she bore down on him. His thumb found her clit and pushed on it. "You like that? Does that feel good? Hmm? Tell me what you like, Amy."

"Yes...so good...yeah, just like that...oh, God, Brett."

Her entire body tensed in his arms, and he held her tight as he continued to work his finger inside of her and on her clit. She once again brought her mouth down on his and kissed him hard, biting at his lips and tongue, as she came all over his hand. Amy gasped and panted. Tremors worked through her body, easing her down from the cliff of pleasure he'd had her suspended on.

Brett brought his finger to her lips. She took it into her mouth and sucked on it. He groaned. Knowing she was sucking the taste of her release from his finger was just plain, fucking hot.

"Come here," he growled, pulling her mouth to his and kissing her. "God damn, you taste so fucking good." He traced her lips with his tongue.

Amy reached between them and freed his cock from his boxer shorts. "I want you, Brett. I need you...on me, in me...please."

It was hard to concentrate on anything when she had her hand wrapped around his cock, stroking it. Fingering her had made him hard. Tasting her from her own lips had made him even harder. Her touching him – he was ready to explode.

"Is this what you want?" Brett pulled her panties to the side and pressed the head of his cock to her opening, but he didn't enter her.

"Yes!"

"Say it." He told her he was going to tease her until she begged for his cock. Well, that time had arrived. "I want to hear you say it."

"I want your cock, Brett. Please, I need it. I need you."

"Then take it, Amy. Take my cock if that's what you want." He expected her to ease down on him as she'd done earlier. But no. She slammed her pussy onto him, causing all the breath in his body to come rushing out. Brett grabbed her hips and held her as she moved on him – up and down, back and forth. "Fucking Christ, your pussy is so wet and hot."

His head fell back to the couch, and his eyes rolled back in his head. Holy shit, she felt more incredible every time he thrust into her. It was apparent from the way she was moving on him that she didn't want slow and easy. She wanted to be fucked.

Brett laid her down on the floor, put her ankles on his shoulders, his hands on either side of her head, and then he fucked her. Hard. Fast. Without mercy.

Amy clutched at his arms as if she wanted him to stop or slow down. But the way she continuously met him thrust for thrust told him otherwise. Her moans were becoming longer, her screams louder. He felt her tightening around him, and he slowed his pace. No woman had ever made him want to come as hard or fast as Amy did. Nor had any woman ever made him want to prolong the inevitable. But with Amy, being inside of her, being this close to her was something he wanted to make last forever.

Brett moved her legs off his shoulders, leaned over to kiss her, and then rolled her on top of him again. He watched the way her head fell back to her shoulders, and her mouth parted on a moan; the way her breasts shook as she rode his cock. Fuck! It was so hot. She was so hot.

"Sonofabitch, Amy...ah, God, baby." He tried to hold her still, to hold off on letting either of them come just yet.

"No." She took his hands from her waist and pinned them above his head. "I need to come again." Amy rotated her hips on him, pushing all the way down on him so that he was buried balls deep inside of her tight, hot pussy. "I want to feel you come inside of me, Brett."

Like he was going to say no to that. He pulled his hands from her grip and wrapped them around her back, holding her firmly against his body as he planted his heels into the floor and fucked her so hard the sounds of their bodies slapping together drowned out their moans.

"Like...that?" he grunted.

His balls were heavy with his impending release; the base of his spine tingled; his body shook, and then he jerked, coming hard and deep inside of her.

Amy nipped and bit at his neck as she gave in to her orgasm. God, the feel of her coming on his cock, of her body going limp on top of his, of her whispering his name at his ear was like heaven on earth. Nothing could be better than this, right here, right now.

"Holy shit," he said on an exhaled breath.

Amy laughed. "Yeah, no kidding."

Brett smoothed the hair from her face and kissed her softly on the mouth. He wanted her again. Now. Always. "God, Amy, you're," he sighed, "you're incredible."

The desire to tell her that he loved her was all-consuming, but he couldn't get the words to form. Was it too soon? Would it freak her out? That's not what he wanted to do, so he kept quiet.

"God, it is so hot in here." Amy rolled off him and onto her back.

"We could take a cold shower," he suggested jokingly.

"You know," she turned her head and looked at him, "that's not a bad idea."

He grinned. "No underwear this time. And I absolutely will not keep my hands to myself."

Amy stood and held her hand out to him. "Good, because I don't want you to."

Brett took her hand and stood. He followed her to the stairs but stopped. "I have a better idea." His cock was already hard again.

At this rate, neither of them would be getting any sleep tonight because he had every intention of spending as much time inside of her as he could.

Chapter Seventeen

B rett pulled out a kitchen chair. "Sit," he said, pointing at it.

"Why?" Amy's voice was full of uncertainty.

With a smile, he said, "Trust me, baby." Then he winked. When she still didn't sit, he pulled her into his arms and kissed her. "Please just trust me. I won't do anything you don't want me to, okay?"

She took a deep breath. "Okay." Amy sat.

"Good. Now don't move." Brett walked into the living room and grabbed her tank top from the floor.

"What are you doing with that?" Her gaze darted from him to the top he held. "Brett...?"

He laughed as he walked around and stood behind her. Lowering his head, he positioned his mouth near her ear. "Relax."

His lips closed around her earlobe, tugging on it gently. Amy moaned and tilted her head to the side, giving him greater access. He dragged his lips from her ear and down her neck, kissing and licking her.

"Amy," he breathed her name as if saying it somehow

made all of this that much more real. Brett straightened and placed the tank top over Amy's eyes, tying it behind her head. She started to stand, but he gently pushed her back down into the chair and leaned close to her ear again. "If you get up again, I will be forced to tie you to the chair."

Amy opened her mouth, but then quickly closed it and simply nodded instead. Brett smiled. He put his hands on her shoulders and ran them down the length of her arms. Lacing his fingers with hers, he brought them around behind her, then released them.

"Keep them there," he instructed.

She nodded again.

Brett went to the refrigerator and took out a bucket of ice. He placed it on the floor next to the chair and stared at Amy for a moment. She was sitting in the chair, blind-folded, hands behind her back, legs spread just enough so he could catch a glimpse of her pussy lips, which glistened with moisture. His cock hardened and then jerked; his hands ached with the need to touch her. Grabbing two pieces of ice from the bucket, he closed his hands around them and then stood behind her again.

"The waiting is killing me." She laughed nervously.

"Put your head back." When she did, he leaned over and captured her lips in a teasing kiss. Keeping his mouth on hers, he reached down and cupped her breasts.

Amy pulled away and gasped. "Holy fuck, Brett, that's cold."

He chuckled and kept his hands on her breasts, holding her firmly in the chair. "You said you were hot, so I figured I'd help cool you down."

"What is that? Ice?"

"Mmm-hmm." Brett walked around and knelt in front

of her. He rubbed the ice around on her nipples and then took them into his mouth one at a time.

"Oh God, Brett." She arched into him and spread her legs open farther.

"Mmm...Your nipples are so hard, Amy." He put the mostly melted ice cubes into his mouth and flicked his thumbs over her nipples. They hardened even more, which only served to arouse him more.

She whispered his name in that needy, seductive way she had about her, and his dick jerked, ready to be buried inside of her. "Please, touch me."

He wanted nothing more than to touch her, but first he was going to tease the living shit out of her, make her so wet and horny for him that she'd beg for him to fuck her. Brett once again leaned forward and took her nipple into his mouth, the ice swirled with his tongue.

Amy wiggled in the chair, her breathing becoming more labored, louder, mixing with her moans. "Brett, I need more, please, give me more."

"More what?" He placed his hands on her knees and ran them up the inside of her thighs, his thumbs meeting at her center and pressing against her clit.

"That...oh...God, yes." She pushed her hips forward, wanting more of him, of his touch. Her head fell back to the chair, and she let out a long, moaning sigh.

The sight of her like that, compliant, ready, spread open for him stole his breath. God, he'd had more than one wet dream about this very thing, about having Amy naked in front of him, about having the freedom to touch her however he wanted. He removed his hands from between her legs and took another piece of ice from the bucket. Popping it into his mouth, he grabbed her thighs and spread her legs. Then he lowered his head and licked her pussy.

Amy gasped again. "More ice?" she whispered.

"Yeah." He sucked her clit into his mouth, and she jerked forward, nearly knocking him backward. "Easy, baby," he crooned. Brett parted her folds and ran a finger down the length of them, pushing his finger deep into her, causing her to moan his name. "You've got such a pretty little pussy," he said as he gripped the ice between his teeth and put it against her clit. Brett let the ice fall from his mouth. All he wanted to do was taste her, make her come.

She wiggled in the chair. "The ice is melting."

He smiled against her. "Come for me, and then you can get out of that chair."

"Fuck," she groaned. Then she speared her fingers into his hair.

Brett pulled his fingers from her and grabbed her hands, pinning them down by her sides. "I told you not to move your hands."

Looked like he'd have to make her come with just his tongue, which was something he was looking forward to. Resuming his position between her legs, he rapidly flicked his tongue over her clit until she was writhing on the chair.

"I want to touch you, Brett...please, let me touch you."

"Uh-uh." He sucked on her clit, drawing it out. "You'll get your chance. But not now."

He closed his eyes and slipped his tongue deep into her pussy, savoring the unique, sweet taste of her. God, he couldn't get past how amazing she tasted, how she made him long to taste only her for the rest of his life.

"Brett," she whimpered.

"Mmm, yeah, that's it, Amy. Come for me, baby. Let me taste you." His tongue was once again working her clit.

Her thighs clenched around his head, making it difficult for him to maneuver, but he knew she was so close to coming. Releasing her hands, he gripped her knees and pried her legs apart. Moments later, she screamed his name as her orgasm tore through her body. He sucked and licked her release until there was none left. Then he lifted his head and rose fully up on his knees.

Amy sat forward and pressed her mouth to his, kissing him hard before he had a chance to say or do anything. He swore his eyes rolled into the back of his head. In all the kisses they'd shared, none had been as hot as this one.

Brett stood and brought Amy to her feet. He lifted her, and she wrapped her legs around his waist, making it very easy for him to slide his cock into her wet pussy. The sensation of being inside of her was so strong it almost brought him to his knees.

He carried her into the living room and laid her on the couch, never once losing contact. Slowly, he removed her blindfold and looked into her eyes. The emotion he saw in them had him stifling a gasp. Was it possible that Amy felt the say way about him? Was this more than just sex to her? God, he hoped so.

"Amy," he whispered, kissing her lips and slowly thrusting into her. Instead of fucking her like he'd planned, he made love to her – slow, passionate love that bonded them in more ways than just the physical.

She wrapped her legs around him and held on to him as if he were the last person on earth, the only man who could ever satisfy her, please her. And he wanted to be that man – the only man to ever see her like this again, the only man to ever touch her and make love to her. She'd agreed to give him more, but how much more? He wanted all of her, forever.

"Brett," she whispered over and over again as she came for the second time.

He allowed himself to let go, to let his own orgasm take over his body as he came hot and hard inside of her – a feeling he didn't know if he'd ever get used to, it was so damn good.

Collapsing on top of her, he kissed her neck and said, "God, I love the sound of my name on your lips."

She laughed softly and whispered his name once more. He shifted his weight and looked down at her, at a loss for words. The only thing that came to his mind was, "I love you," but he knew she wasn't ready to hear that yet. He didn't even know if he was truly ready to say it. Instead, he just kissed her.

Amy lay snuggled to Brett's side, her head on his chest. She traced lazy circles on his stomach, a feeling of calm settled over her. She couldn't believe she was actually having sex with Brett Hudson. The man she'd dreamt of for years. The man she never thought she'd ever have. But now...now she was lying in his arms after the most amazing sex of her life.

"Brett? Are you still awake?"

"Hmm? Yeah." He yawned.

"Are we okay?"

"What? Yeah, of course we are. Why wouldn't we be?"

She shrugged. "I don't know. I'm just worried how this is going to affect our friendship."

Brett put his fingers under her chin and tilted her head up. "Baby, please don't worry about it. We're going to be fine. I promise."

She folded her hands on his chest and rested her chin atop them. "How can you be so sure?"

"Because I refuse to ever let anything come between us."

Amy smiled. His tone was adamant, and she had no reason not to believe him. "Thank you," she whispered.

"Come here." He pulled her up the length of him and slanted his lips over hers, kissing her in that slow, soft, erotic way that she'd grown to love. Brett broke the kiss and licked his lips. "Mmm, I love kissing you."

Her heart fluttered. "I'm afraid that if I close my eyes and sleep that when I wake up, all of this will just be a dream."

Brett smiled and gave her another chaste kiss. "It's okay, Amy." He laughed. "Go to sleep, baby, and I'll be right here when you wake up, holding you." He squeezed her tighter to him and she sighed with contentment. Settling next to him, she closed her eyes and succumbed to sleep.

Chapter Eighteen

Amy's heart thundered in her chest and ears as the boat slowed and dropped anchor.

Brett squeezed her hand and smiled. "Relax, it'll be fun," he said.

Fun? Yeah, right. She was seriously reconsidering her decision to go scuba diving with Brett. He'd literally begged her last night and when it came to Brett Hudson, she just couldn't tell him no – especially when it was something he really wanted to do. Plus, he'd been so sweet to her all week, making more than one of her fantasies a reality. So, after a rather intense session of love making, she'd agreed. And even though she was terrified, she did want to do this for him.

They'd spent all morning in a class that taught them everything they needed to know. It still didn't calm Amy's nerves any. There were quite a few people on the boat who'd never dived before, so she was in good company. It's not like she was a novice among a group of experienced divers. And she had been sure to ask a ton of questions about the safety procedures for ensuring everyone was on the boat before going back to the island.

Everything would be fine.

Besides, Brett promised to stay by her side the entire time, and she trusted him completely. One by one, people stood, put on their masks and mouthpieces, and then jumped into the ocean.

When it came to their turn, Amy sat, paralyzed with fear. "I don't think I can do this," she said.

Brett crouched in front of her and put his hands on her knees. "Look at me, baby." Slowly, she lifted her gaze to meet his. He smiled. "You can do this. I know you can."

"Uh-uh." She shook her head adamantly.

"I will be by your side the entire time." He kissed her softly on the cheek and whispered, "Trust me."

"I do," she said.

"Then you know I'd never let anything happen to you, right?"

"Yeah."

"And if a shark does attack, I'll offer myself up for bait, okay?"

Amy laughed. "If you do that, you'll be breaking your promise to stay by my side."

It was his turn to laugh. "Okay, then I guess we're both getting eaten." He winked.

She stood and nodded. "All right, let's go get eaten by a shark."

"That's my girl."

The smile that formed on her face couldn't be contained. That's right. She was his girl! And dammit, she wouldn't let him down.

Twenty minutes later, they were a hundred feet deep in the ocean surrounded by the most colorful, vibrant sea life she'd ever seen. During their instructional class, they were shown images of the various types of fish and coral they would encounter. So far, Amy had seen six different species of fish, each one more awe inspiring than the previous.

Brett grabbed her shoulder and pointed at something off to her left – a Spotted Eagle ray. Wow! It was beautiful and graceful. It floated by them as if they weren't even there. Brett gave her a thumbs up, and then motioned for her to follow him.

She did, and they encountered a breathtaking coral landscape. A school of grayish colored fish swam within reaching distance from them. Amy was so glad that Brett talked her into doing this. She was even happier that they hadn't encountered a single shark or jellyfish.

He took her hand, and they made their way up to the surface. Once on the boat and out of their gear, Brett pulled her into his arms and kissed her. "My God, that was amazing wasn't it?"

Amy laughed at this excitement. "Yes, it was pretty friggin' amazing," she agreed.

They took their seats and waited as everyone else climbed aboard. A final head count was done, and then the boat headed back toward the island.

Brett took Amy's hand and gave her knuckles a kiss. "It's our last night here. What do you want to do?" he asked.

She'd be happy spending it in bed with him. "I don't care. Whatever you want."

"We'll go out," he said.

Now that the power was restored, normal activities on the island had resumed and as much fun as it was spending the past couple of days in bed, she was excited to be able to get out and do stuff again.

Brett stood by the bar with Jason, sipping a beer while Amy and Emma danced to the island band's unique music. Brett hadn't taken his eyes off Amy all night. She looked downright gorgeous in that flowery, blue sundress. She'd left her hair down and pulled back one side by tucking a large, white flower into it.

"You're a lucky man, Brett." Jason patted him on the back. "She's a beautiful woman."

"I know," he said, keeping his gaze focused on Amy.

The way she moved her body to the music entranced him. Her movements were graceful, elegant, seductive. He wondered if she realized just how sexy she was, or how many men she had watching her. It didn't bother Brett too much that other men were staring at Amy because he knew that she was all his, that it would be his bed and his arms that she would be in tonight – And every other night for the rest of their lives, too, if he had his way.

His cell phone rang, momentarily distracting him. He pulled it from his pocket, expecting it to be his mom checking in again. It wasn't. It was Vanessa.

Brett's finger hesitated over the answer button. She'd been calling twice a day every day since the wedding. He should just answer and get it over with. Tell her that he wasn't angry with her and that he wished her the best in life. But then he glanced up and saw a man talking to Amy.

The man repeatedly tried to reach for Amy, to touch her, and each time she'd shake her head and pull away from him.

Oh, hell no! Looking was one thing. Touching was another. Brett quickly rejected the call and approached Amy. He put his arm around her waist and pulled her to him. "Is there a problem here?"

Amy looked relieved to see him. She put one hand on his lower back and the other on his chest. "No, there's no problem." She smiled at him.

"Yeah, no problem here." The man slowly backed up with his hands in the air.

Brett continued to glare at him until he turned and walked away. "Are you okay? He looked like he was grabbing at you."

"I'm fine," she assured him. "Thanks for coming to my rescue though."

He pulled her to his chest as if they were dancing but kissed her instead. "Anything for you, baby."

She smiled against his lips and then kissed him again. "You haven't danced with me all night."

"I was waiting for the right song," he said as he began to move around the dance floor with her. "Besides, I was having fun watching you dance with Emma."

Amy gave him a strange look. "That's not some sick guy fantasy about lesbians, is it?"

Brett laughed. "No." He spun her around and then yanked her tight to his body. "I just like watching you dance. Always have."

"Always?" Her voice was full of disbelief.

He nodded. "You're very sexy, Amy. I don't think you realize the effect you have on men."

She rolled her eyes.

"I'm serious. There wasn't a single man in here that didn't have his eyes on you earlier."

"I think you're exaggerating."

He simply smiled and shook his head. That was the difference between Amy and Vanessa. Vanessa knew she was beautiful and used it to her advantage, whereas Amy didn't realize. Or if she did, she didn't try to flaunt it, which only made her more desirable in his eyes.

"Were your eyes on me, too?" she asked playfully.

Brett pulled her closer and put his mouth near her ear. "I haven't stopped looking at you since we got here." He felt her breath hitch when he kissed right below her ear.

The slow music they were dancing to switched to something faster, more energetic. "I need a cold drink," she said, fanning her face with her hand.

Taking her hand, Brett led her to the bar and ordered her a glass of Dom Perignon and an ice water. He stood by her side, hand on the small of her back, and watched as she sipped the champagne.

She reached into her water, grabbed a piece of ice, and rubbed it around her neck like she'd done that night at Nefarious. And it had the same exact effect on him, too. Worse, actually, since every time he saw a piece of ice all he could think of was Amy in that chair, him licking her with ice in his mouth.

Brett kissed her temple and whispered, "Watching you do that is making my cock rock hard." He'd learned very quickly that Amy enjoyed dirty talk. Lucky for him, he did, too.

She gave him a seductive little smile. "So, it probably won't help to know that I'm not wearing any panties."

He lowered his hand from her back to her ass – definitely no panties. He groaned. "C'mon, I think it's time to leave."

Amy laughed. "I think you're right."

Chapter Nineteen

Amy waited as Brett spread the blanket on the ground, and then she sat between his legs. He'd woken her at the ass crack of dawn and brought her back to the same secluded spot he'd brought her that day for the picnic. At first, she was annoyed that he'd woken her so early when they'd spent the entire night making love, and she was exhausted, but now that she was wrapped up in his arms, watching the sunrise over the ocean, she was no longer annoyed.

Brett nuzzled her neck and kissed the sensitive spot behind her ear. She sighed with contentment and snuggled deeper into his arms. "Thank you for getting up and coming here with me. Even if you are grumpy."

She playfully elbowed him. "I'm not grumpy, I'm tired. Someone kept me up all night."

"Are you complaining?"

"Never." She smiled and turned her face toward him for a kiss, which he willingly gave to her. Like she would ever complain about being with him. "Can I ask you a question?"

"Of course." But he kissed her again before she had a

chance to speak. "You can always ask me anything. You know that."

"We leave in few hours, Brett. What happens when we get home?" Amy adjusted her body so that her back was to his chest again. She didn't want him to see the fear in her eyes. "With us," she added as an afterthought, "what happens with us?"

"Well..." He took both of her hands into his and laced their fingers together. "For starters, dinner at my parents' house."

She laughed. "Other than that?"

"I want you to move in with me, Amy." He said it so calmly, like it was no big deal, but his words echoed in her ears.

Move in with him? She had to bite down on the inside of her cheek to stop from squealing with delight. "Wouldn't it be better if you moved in with me?"

Amy owned a house, whereas Brett rented a very large apartment. She had nothing against apartment living, and honestly, she'd live in a box with Brett if he asked her to, but it seemed like a step backward to sell her house and move into his apartment.

"Then I'll move in with you."

"Really?" That seemed a little too easy.

"Yes, really." He chuckled. "I don't care where we call home as long as I get to make love to you every night and wake up with you by my side every day."

"Aww," she cooed, turning her head to kiss him again. "That's the sweetest thing anyone has ever said to me."

"Give me time. I'm sure I can come up with something better." He winked.

Amy once again turned her gaze back to the rising sun. Other than saying, "I love you," she really didn't think he would be able to top that. Closing her eyes, she rested her head on his chest and enjoyed being in his arms, which, in her opinion, was exactly where she'd always belonged.

After several moments of silence, she asked, "Why were you going to marry Vanessa when you'd only known her for six months?"

Behind her, Brett sighed. "I don't know. I guess I was caught up in the excitement of the show and how we'd met. She was so full of life, and she wanted the same things I did. At least, she said she did. It was apparent after my bachelor party that her future plans left no room for my friendship with you."

"She knew that you were with me the night of your bachelor party?"

"Yeah, I don't know how she found out, but she did. And she threw a vase at my head."

Amy laughed, then cupped her hand over her mouth. "I'm sorry, that's really not funny."

Brett squeezed her tighter against him. "It kind of is."

"So, if you knew she wanted different things, why didn't you call off the engagement?"

"I probably should have, but I truly believed I could change her mind about you."

It hurt to sit there and hear Brett talk about Vanessa like that. And it really hurt to know that he was willing to marry a woman who wanted to completely cut Amy out of his life. Sure, Brett was with her now, but if Vanessa hadn't left him at the altar...the thought brought tears to her eyes. She drew a shaky breath and swallowed the dryness from her throat.

"It would've been a mistake to marry her. I know that now," he said.

Yeah, he realized that now, but what would he have done had he actually married her? Amy tried to push the thoughts from her mind. She didn't want to ruin the morning or their last few hours on this beautiful island by having all these depressing thoughts.

"Amy?"

"Yeah?"

Brett put his hand on the side of her face and turned her to look at him. "Vanessa is a non-issue. I've always said that everything happens for a reason, and I have to believe that Vanessa leaving me at the altar was so that I could find you."

Amy remained silent, hating the fact that her eyes were wet with unshed tears. She didn't know what the hell was wrong with her. They'd spent all night last night making love; then this morning he brought her here to watch the sunrise, and all she could do was mope about the fact that he'd almost married another woman. God, she was an idiot. She should just accept the fact that fate or God or whatever other powers that be stepped in and finally gave her a chance with Brett.

"Hey," he said so softly she almost didn't hear him despite being so close. Brett gave her lips a lingering, tongue-less kiss. "I'm so hopelessly in love with you, Amy."

All at once, her heart stopped beating, her breath caught in her throat, and tears spilled down her cheeks. Brett loved her? Oh God! *He loves me!* Amy turned and knelt between his legs so that she was fully facing him.

"I love you, too, Brett. So much." Those last two words came out more as a sob.

He smiled. "You're mine now, Amy, and I have no intentions of letting you go."

"I want to pinch myself to make sure I'm not dreaming."

Brett laughed. "Trust me, you're not dreaming."

She pressed her mouth to his and kissed him hard enough to push him down on his back. He put one hand on the back of her head and slipped the other down her shorts, onto her ass, pulling her against his growing erection.

"Make love to me," she said against his lips.

"Here?" He was already working her shorts down her hips and thighs.

"Yes, here." Amy lifted her body enough to accommodate his efforts. "It's secluded. No one will see us." She was glad she'd been too tired this morning to bother finding a pair of panties to put on.

Brett rolled her onto her back, yanked his shirt off over his head, and then removed his shorts. She reached out, trailed a finger down his torso, and along his shaft. His cock jerked under her touch, and she smiled. It was surreal to know she now had access to him whenever she wanted. All she had to do was ask, and he would do anything she wanted.

He reached down and caressed her breast. "You are so beautiful."

His hand continued downward over her ribs and stomach, sending a thousand tiny shivers through her body, stopping once he reached her folds, which he ran a finger between.

Amy moaned softly and lifted her hips, encouraging him to slide that finger into her. But he didn't. Instead, he continued to rub it along her folds, stopping every so often to rub her clit. Her breathing was becoming labored, and she felt that wonderful tingle in her body. It started deep in her core and slowly spread to her legs and toes, her arms and face. Her fingers felt numb.

"Brett," she whimpered.

Finally, he plunged a finger deep into her, and she cried out, on the verge of orgasm already. Christ, the things he did to her. Then, just as quickly, he removed his finger from her. Damn him! Capturing her lips, he kissed her long and hard as he settled between her legs and entered her.

As his cock sunk into her, his moan was deep and low at her ear. "Holy fuck, I swear you feel better and better every time."

"Yes." She tucked her legs around his, hooking her feet under his ass and meeting him thrust for thrust. At first, his movements were fast, almost frantic, as if he needed to get out years' worth of pent-up sexual frustration, but then he slowed down and really took his time.

Brett rested his forearms on either side of her head, smoothing the hair from her forehead. His kiss matched the tempo of his cock moving in and out of her – slow, steady, controlled, yet totally hot. It drove her insane when he made love to her like that. He'd done it last night, too, and she'd come so hard she almost passed out from the force of it.

"Open your eyes," he whispered. When she didn't, he stopped moving, and said, "Amy, baby, please open your eyes for me."

Amy forced her eyes open and looked into Brett's gorgeous baby blues. There was so much love and passion in his eyes it almost brought her to tears again.

"That's better." He smiled and started to move in and out of her again, giving her exactly what she wanted.

As far as sex went, Amy wasn't shy or inexperienced, but this – making love with her eyes open, her gaze locked with Brett's – was new. And she decided very quickly that she liked it. A lot. It was a new level of intimacy she'd never felt or shared before.

"Brett." God...he was destroying her. If he ever left her, or stopped loving her, or wasn't her friend anymore, she would never survive it. Never.

"You're mine, Amy." He increased his pace, his cock swelling inside of her. "All mine."

"Yes." She felt her orgasm building in her toes and making its way to her core.

"I love you," he whispered.

That's when she lost control. Hearing Brett say those words to her were a dream come true, but to have him say it while making love to her was surreal.

"I love you, too," she said.

Moments later, they both succumbed to the pleasure only they could give each other.

Brett collapsed on top of her, and she lazily stroked his sweat dampened hair. Amy had never been so happy in her entire life. She yawned, content to fall asleep right there on the beach with him on top of her. It would be hard leaving the island. Once they got back home, there would be work and other distractions. It wouldn't be just the two of them anymore. A few tears slipped past her defenses and down her face.

"Hey," he put his weight into his arms and looked down at her, "why are you crying?"

She hastily wiped her tears. "I don't know. I guess I'm just sad about leaving."

"Will it help if I promise you that things won't change between us?" He smiled.

"Maybe a little." She laughed halfheartedly.

His intentions were sincere, but she knew that things would change. There was no way they couldn't. Hopefully, their feelings for each other wouldn't, though.

Chapter Twenty

Brett sat on the back porch of his parents' house with his brother. Amy was inside with his mom, and his father was in the yard fighting to get the grill lit. Brett and Amy had arrived home late last night and crashed at her house.

Well, that wasn't completely accurate. It was more like they barely got inside before they started tearing at each other's clothes. Then they made love until they collapsed from physical exhaustion. All morning and most of the afternoon were spent sleeping, and then they made love some more before showering – together – and getting ready for dinner with his parents.

"So, how many days were you on that island before you started tapping that?" Craig asked, tilting his beer bottle toward the kitchen window where Amy could be seen.

Brett sighed. "Don't start this again, Craig. I told you. Amy and I are just friends." His heart raced.

The last thing he needed or wanted was for his brother to start prying. Brett and Amy had agreed to keep their relationship a secret from his parents for the time being because he knew once they told his mother, she would have their wedding planned and their babies named before dinner was on the table. And neither of them wanted to deal with that just yet. They simply wanted to enjoy each other for a while longer. In his mind, he was still on that island, and it was all about him and her. He wasn't ready to face reality, to have the real world barge in on them and steal them away from each other.

"I thought for sure you two would've hooked up." Craig brought his beer to his lips and took a drink. "Not even one drunken night?"

"Nope." Brett shook his head.

"Huh. Well, if you're not going to make a move on Amy, then I will. She's a catch, little bro."

Brett glared at his brother. "You want Amy?" Over his dead fucking body would Craig ever get his hands on Amy.

"What man wouldn't?"

Stay calm. Brett took a deep breath. He eyed his brother with disdain. Was Craig being serious, or was he just trying to trick Brett into admitting there was something going on with Amy? Either scenario was a real possibility. Then again, Amy and Craig had gotten close while Brett was away for the show. It could be a real possibility that Craig liked her.

"Since when have you had a thing for Amy?" Brett asked.

Craig shrugged. "I've always thought she was hot, but while you were gone, I really got to know her. She's cool. It wasn't until I saw her at your wedding that I thought, 'Wow, I could see myself with her.' And then when you said there was nothing between the two of you..." He trailed off.

Brett inhaled deeply through his nose and exhaled slowly through his mouth. "Are you fucking with me right now?"

"No." Craig laughed.

"You're not her type." Brett finished his beer and slammed it down on the table with more force than necessary.

"Maybe we should let her decide that."

Brett clenched his hands into fists and then flexed them. He would not let his brother goad him into saying anything. He knew Amy loved him, and that she was his. So, even if his brother did try to make a move on her, she would reject him. But...the thought of his brother looking at Amy in that way, thinking of her like that...it made his blood boil.

"In fact, I think I'll ask her out right now." Craig stood.

Brett grabbed his arm and stood, getting in his face. "Amy is off limits to you."

"And why's that?" Craig smiled.

Brett narrowed his eyes at him and scowled.

"I knew it." Craig poked Brett in the chest. "You two are hooking up, aren't you?"

Brett hushed him. "Keep your voice down. We don't want Mom to know just yet."

Craig whistled. "So, tell me, how long did it take you?"

With a smile of pure male satisfaction, Brett said, "Two days."

"Well, it's about damn time." Craig laughed.

Brett shook his head. "I mean it, Craig. She's off limits, and I swear to God if you tell Mom, I will kill you."

"Whoa, easy. I'm not gonna tell Mom anything." Craig patted Brett on the back. "Seriously though, I'm glad you pulled your head out of your ass. You and Amy are good together."

Brett couldn't contain his smile. "I know."

Now that he was agitated, there was only one thing that could calm him down. Too bad for him, he couldn't walk up to Amy, pull her into his arms, and devour her lips like he wanted to. This dinner couldn't be over soon enough.

"So, when are you two getting married?" Craig asked.

"We haven't even talked about it," Brett said, keeping his gaze on the kitchen window and Amy. "We're just enjoying being together right now."

"Don't fuck this up, Brett." Craig patted Brett on the shoulder.

No, Brett had no intentions of fucking things up with Amy. He'd never be able to live with himself if he did.

Amy stood idly by and watched as Brett's mom prepared dinner. "Are you sure there's nothing I can do to help?"

"Yes, I'm sure." Ginny chopped some more onions and tossed them into the homemade spaghetti sauce that was cooking on the stove. "You can help by telling me how Brett's doing. That boy has never liked to talk to me about these types of things."

Amy knew this was coming. She took a calming breath. "I assure you he's doing fine. He's realized that marrying Vanessa would've been a mistake."

"Well, thank heavens for that." Ginny wiped her hands

on her apron and set the knife in the sink. "And how are you doing?"

Okay, that question threw Amy for a loop. She'd expected Ginny to ask about Brett and how he was doing. She did not expect her to ask about Amy. "Uh, I'm okay. Tired. That jet lag is a real killer." She laughed nervously.

"I remember the flight to Japan that Dean and I took. It took me weeks to recuperate from that. Lots of rest." Ginny smiled.

Amy nodded. That was easier said than done. Now that Brett would be living with her, rest wasn't high on her priority list. The sound of the doorbell prevented her from responding.

"Would you mind getting that?" Ginny asked Amy. "I have to get these noodles on the stove."

"Sure." Amy walked to the door and opened it. She came face to face with Vanessa. Amy's stomach felt like it had dropped to the floor. "Uh, hi."

"Oh, Amy, I didn't realize...I was...is Brett here?"

Amy wanted to scream at Vanessa to go away, to shout at her that she had her chance and blew it, and that Brett had moved on. But she didn't.

Instead, she nodded. "I'll go get him for you."

The walk from the front door to the back porch was the longest walk of her life. She was afraid that if she let Brett talk to Vanessa, he would change his mind about everything, that he would realize he still loved Vanessa and didn't want to be with Amy. That thought had tears burning her eyes and throat. She should've known that this was inevitable, that Brett would have to talk to Vanessa sooner or later. She'd just hoped it would be later...much, much later.

"Brett, there's someone here to see you," Amy whispered, having trouble getting the words past her lips.

Brett stood and walked up to Amy. She was shocked when he put his hand on her waist and put his mouth to her ear, which he kissed softly. Amy closed her eyes and fought to hold back her tears. "It's okay. Craig knows. He promised to keep it a secret. I'll explain later."

Amy nodded, not wanting to tell him who was outside waiting for him, not wanting him to let her go. But she had to. "Vanessa's here to see you."

He jerked away and looked at her, his eyes wide with shock.

Amy simply nodded, and then said, "She's outside." She put her head down, unable to look him in the eyes.

Brett put his finger under her chin and tilted her head up. He placed a quick, chaste kiss to her lips, then whispered, "I love you, Amy. You're the only woman I want. And that's exactly what I'm going to tell her. Okay?"

Amy nodded and then watched as Brett walked away from her and toward Vanessa. Amy blew out a shaky breath.

"You don't have anything to worry about," Craig said from behind her.

She'd forgotten he was there. Turning to face him, she smiled weakly, and said, "I know." But she didn't know. She was terrified that seeing Vanessa and talking to her would change his mind.

"Seriously, Amy, you really don't," he said.

Amy took a seat next to him and tried to distract herself from thinking about Brett and Vanessa. It worked for a little while, but the minutes ticked by, and ten minutes turned into half an hour. She was ready to jump out of her skin. When she simply couldn't take it any longer, she got up and went outside to check on them.

When she opened the door, she saw Brett holding Vanessa's face in his hands, and he was pulling away, as if he'd just finished kissing her. Amy's heart shattered into a million pieces. Brett was kissing Vanessa? Amy cupped her hand over her mouth to stifle a gasp. She would not let him know how much he'd just hurt her.

"I don't mean to interrupt," Amy said as she walked down the steps and up to where Brett and Vanessa stood, "but I just wanted to let you know that I'm leaving. Have a nice evening."

"What? Wait." Brett released Vanessa and grabbed Amy's wrist. "Where are you going?"

"To see Lucy."

"Your sister's boyfriend drama can wait," he said.

Amy yanked her arm out of his grasp. She looked over his shoulder at Vanessa, and then back at him. "I'd much rather deal with Lucy's boyfriend drama than my own. I'm sure it'll hurt a lot less."

Brett recoiled as if she'd slapped him. "What the hell does that mean?"

"I saw you just now, Brett. You were kissing her."

"What? No, I wasn't. Amy, please, just calm down and let me explain."

Amy shook her head. "Did you tell her?" She crossed her arms over her chest. "Huh? Did you?" When he still didn't answer, she said, "Did you tell Vanessa that you were in love with me? That you've moved on and want to be with me?" Amy didn't care that she was shouting, or that Brett's parents probably heard everything she'd just said.

"Not yet," he said softly.

Not yet? He'd been out here with her for half an hour. What the hell had they been doing? Oh, that's right. He was too busy kissing her. Amy lost the battle to keep her tears locked away.

"Don't bother." Amy spun on her heel and walked away. She hoped, expected, Brett to follow her. He didn't.

By the time Amy got to the end of the street, she was sobbing so hard she couldn't walk any farther. How could Brett have done this to her?

Chapter Twenty-One

"Fuck!" Brett dragged a hand through his hair. He turned back to Vanessa. "I think it's time for you to leave."

"Is it true?" She took a step toward him. "What she just said...is it true?"

"Yes." From the corner of his eye, he saw his parents and his brother standing on the front porch. Looked like the secret was out, he thought as he took a deep breath. "I'm in love with Amy, and she's the woman I want to spend my life with. I'm sorry if that hurts you, Vanessa, but I want you to know that I'm not angry with you for what you did."

Then he turned and ran after Amy, shouting her name.

Brett rounded the corner, but Amy wasn't there. Where the hell could she have gone? He fumbled to get his cell phone out of his pocket and called her. It went straight to voicemail. He hung up and called right back. Voicemail again. Brett continued to call as he walked back toward his parents' house. All his calls went unanswered.

"Fuck!" he shouted again.

Not only did Brett have to make things right with Amy,

he had to find her first, and he was now going to have to face his parents – alone. This was not how he wanted to tell them. This was not how he expected this night would go. God, all he wanted was Amy, right here, right now. He wanted to pull her into his arms and kiss her, tell her how much he loved her. Christ, how did he manage to fuck this up already?

"Brett Matthew Hudson...what the—"

"Not now, Mom," he said as he opened his car door and got inside. Right now, he had to find Amy. He'd deal with his mother's questions later.

Brett awoke with a start. He rubbed his eyes and yawned, trying to get his bearings. He'd gone to Amy's house – their house – and waited for Amy to arrive. She never did. Brett stood and stretched. It was almost nine in the morning. He knew she would be at the studio; they were resuming classes today. Brett grabbed his keys from the coffee table and rushed out of the house.

He arrived at the studio fifteen minutes later. Sure enough, Amy was there. He took a moment to watch her as she instructed the group of students. She looked tired, sad, and her eyes were bloodshot, as if she'd spent the night crying. The thought that she had, and that he'd been the cause of it, sickened him. He would make things right. He had to because life without Amy wasn't worth living.

"Dylan, you look like an overcooked noodle today," Amy said, her heels clicking against the floor as she made her way toward the boy. Her voice snapped Brett out of his thoughts. "Do you need the posture bar?"

"No, Miss Amy," Dylan responded, straightening his back. His arms were still all wrong.

Brett used the opportunity to his advantage. He walked up to Dylan and repositioned his arms, putting his hand on the boy's back to straighten him the proper way. Then he locked his gaze with Amy's. She looked at him for only a moment before averting her gaze, but not before Brett noticed the unshed tears in her eyes.

"Okay," Amy said, "one more time. Five, six, seven, eight...turn, turn, turn...good. Nice job, Mindy, great lines."

Brett stood next to her and watched the students dance. "I'm sorry," he said.

"You're late. Classes start promptly at nine," she said without looking at him. "Vanessa keep you up too late last night?"

There was so much venom in her voice. "I wasn't with Vanessa," he said angrily. "I spent the entire night at *our* house waiting for you to come home."

She still wouldn't look at him.

He sighed. "Amy, please, just talk to me."

"Nice job, guys," she said, clapping her hands and smiling at the students. "Okay, take five, and then we'll work on some new choreography." Finally, she looked at him. "You want me to talk? Fine, I'll talk."

She ushered him into the corner and lowered her voice to an angry whisper. "I have spent my entire life loving you, Brett. You're the only person in the world I have ever completely trusted, and last night you broke my heart and destroyed my trust in you. There's no coming back from that."

They stood in a silent battle of wills. He knew he'd hurt her, but he hadn't realized how much. He also knew that if he didn't do something, he would lose her forever. And that wasn't an option.

Brett swallowed hard. "You're wrong."

He turned and walked away. He would come back from this, and he knew exactly how he was going to do it, too.

Amy sighed with aggravation when her cell phone rang again. This time, it was a text message from Brett. At least he'd moved on from calling every four seconds.

BRETT: Emergency at the studio. Come now! Urgent! 911.

She didn't even think twice about it. Amy was out of her sister's apartment and rushing toward her car. Her thoughts raced. Was the studio on fire? Had it been vandalized? Burglarized? Why hadn't she been notified? She was listed as the owner, too, so why hadn't the police called her?

When she arrived, the building looked fine. There were no signs of anything bad. But the lights were on. She got out of her car and went inside.

Brett stood in the middle of the room. Why the fuck did he have to look so damn sexy? And why was her first thought to go to him and throw herself into his arms? She'd give anything to be back on that island with him right now.

"What the hell is going on?" she asked. "What's wrong with the studio?"

"Nothing, I needed to get you here and this was the only way I knew how," Brett said.

"I'm leaving." She turned to do just that when something caught her eye. "Is that a pile of sand on the floor?" Her voice got progressively louder with each spoken word. "Why is there sand on my dance floor?" He knew how neurotic she was about a clean floor.

"I can explain." He smiled, and she felt her knees get weak.

Amy crossed her arms over her chest and impatiently tapped her foot. "Well...I'm waiting?"

He licked his lips, and she cursed herself for watching him, wanting him. "Do you remember our last day on the island? We watched the sunrise on the beach?"

"Yes." That was the day he'd told her he loved her, and then they made love. She would never forget that day for as long as she lived.

Brett walked up to her and gently rubbed his hands up and down her arms. The contact sent her body into a tailspin. "In those seconds before I told you I loved you, I had a moment of perfect clarity. Everything suddenly made sense to me. Our relationship, my feelings for you, my life..." He shook his head.

Amy remained silent, knowing if she tried to speak, she would just end up crying.

"Remember prom?" Brett reached into his pocket and pulled something out. He pushed a button on it and a picture of them at prom popped up against the window shades.

That's when Amy realized he'd set up a laptop that was projecting onto the closed shades covering the windows. "Yeah, I remember prom."

How could she forget? She'd turned down two invitations, one from the most popular boy in school, because she'd been waiting for Brett to ask her. When he finally did, it wasn't anything like she'd thought it would be.

"I gave you some lame excuse about not wanting to go, but my mom was making me. I asked you to go with me so that I didn't have to take a real date."

Yup. That's exactly how he'd asked her, too, and it had hurt more than she thought possible.

"Then there was Jenna Lewis' graduation party." He pushed the button again, and another picture of them popped up. "Blamed this one on my mom, too." Brett smiled and quickly clicked through several more pictures. "Hundreds of frat parties in college. Craig's college graduation. Aunt Linda's retirement party. My parents' twenty-fifth wedding anniversary. Dozens of family reunions. That ridiculous Christmas party at my dad's company that he made me go to."

Every time a new picture was displayed, Amy was bombarded with memories of each specific event. She'd begun crying after the prom picture and hadn't stopped. She made no attempt to hide her tears, either. There was no point.

"And then, of course, there was my recent honeymoon."

An aerial photo of the island filled her vision, and she lost it. She put her hand over her mouth and sobbed so hard her shoulders shook. Thankfully, Brett didn't try to touch her, because that would've only made things worse.

He tucked the plastic button device back in his pocket and continued to speak. "I have a bad habit of giving you lame excuses to get you to go places with me. And I finally know why."

"Why?" She wasn't sure she really wanted to know, but the question had been asked.

"Because I was too damn scared to just ask you out. I've had so many opportunities, and I've missed every single one of them because I'm scared shitless, Amy. I'm scared of how I feel about you. I'm scared of ruining our friendship. I'm scared that you might not feel the same way about me."

She didn't know what to say to that. It's not like they could go back in time and have a do-over. Nothing he said could change what had already happened between them. But the urge to grab him and tell him that he had nothing to be scared of was overwhelming.

"But this," he pointed to the window shades as another picture popped up, "this is the moment I regret the most."

It was a beautiful picture of that secluded beach where they'd watched the sunrise. Amy closed her eyes, not wanting to relive that moment. It hurt too much to know she'd been so close to having the life with Brett she'd always dreamed of and knowing she'd lost it.

Brett took her hand and laced their fingers together. "Go back there with me, Amy." He pointed to the picture again. "Let me have that moment back so that I can say what I should've said back then."

She never could say no to him. With a nod, she let Brett lead her to the pile of sand. Just like that morning, she sat between his legs and rested her head on his chest. He wrapped his arms around her, and when she closed her eyes, she was back on that beach with him. She could feel the light breeze on her face. She could smell the remnants of the rainstorm from a few nights before. She could hear the ocean as it rolled onto the shore. She could feel his hot breath on her neck. And she could feel his heart beating in his chest.

Brett nuzzled her neck and then kissed it. A fresh wave of tears streamed down her face. "You have spent your life loving me, and I've spent my life choosing you. Every event that I could've taken a girlfriend to, I chose to take you. Every girlfriend that ever said, 'Brett, it's me or Amy,' I've always chosen you."

"Except for Vanessa," she choked out the words in between sobs.

Brett clutched her chin in his thumb and forefinger and turned her face toward him. "Especially Vanessa," he said.

Amy's lips trembled. The look in his eyes was so intense, so full of truth it stunned her.

"Did you know that when the music started and everyone turned to watch Vanessa walk down the aisle, I was looking at you?"

"No." Amy shook her head. If it was his goal to make her blubber like a baby, he was doing a damn good job. Every time he spoke, she would cry harder.

"I was. And I knew that I couldn't marry her because it would mean giving you up. I'd made up my mind that if she had actually come walking down that aisle, I wasn't going to go through with it. I couldn't. I couldn't give you up. I knew that I was going to choose you again."

She desperately wanted to believe him. Was it possible he was telling her the truth? He looked like he was. But...what about last night? Why hadn't he told Vanessa about them like he said he would? She opened her mouth to ask, but he spoke before she had a chance.

"I've always chosen you, Amy. Always. And now I'm

asking you to choose me." He kissed her softly on the lips, and she whimpered a little when he pulled away. Brett held a diamond ring in his hand. Amy stared at it for a moment, then looked at him. "Choose me to be the man you spend the rest of your life loving. Choose me to be the father of your children and your husband."

"Oh my God," she whispered, turning around so that her back was to his chest again. Was this really happening? Was Brett seriously proposing to her? She needed a moment to collect herself.

"Amy, look at me, baby, please." He turned her so that she had to look at him. Using his free hand, he wiped away her tears with his thumb. "I love you so much, and I don't want to live a life that you're not a part of. Will you marry me?"

"Yes," she said before he even finished the question. "Yes, a million times yes."

Brett slipped the ring on her finger and smiled. Amy held out her hand to admire the ring. It was simple, but gorgeous. And it was Brett's ring!

"I wanted to ask you that morning on the beach, but I chickened out."

"This way was so much better." She laughed.

"I'm so sorry about last night."

"It looked like you were kissing her."

"I wasn't. I swear. She tried to kiss me, but I wouldn't let her. What you saw was me pushing her away."

Amy flung her arms around Brett and buried her face in his neck. "I love you."

He hugged her so tight it was hard to breathe, but she didn't care. She was in Brett's arms, and he was now her fiancé. He could do whatever the hell he wanted so long as he was doing it to her or with her.

"I love you, too, Amy, so much." He kissed her neck. "Can we go home now? Together?"

"Yes." She released him and looked into his piercing blue eyes. "Take me home and make love to me, Brett."

Chapter Twenty-Two

Brett lay in bed next to Amy and watched her sleep. He stroked her hair. She agreed to marry him! When he'd planned that whole thing at the studio, he had serious doubts that it would actually work. And when she'd barely said anything, and just stood there crying, he really didn't think it would work. But she'd said yes and that's all that mattered. Amy would be his wife.

He leaned over and kissed her forehead. "I love you," he whispered.

"I love you," she said.

"I thought you were sleeping."

Amy rolled over to face him. "No, I can't stop staring at my ring." She laughed.

He smiled. "I'm glad you like it."

"Like it? Are you kidding? I love it." She put her hand on his cheek and leaned up to kiss him. "I'm never taking it off."

"Good." Brett gently pushed her onto her back and brought his body over hers, spreading her legs and settling between them.

He didn't enter her, but he did push his erection against her, letting her know that he wanted her again. The urgency he'd felt on the island disappeared. Now that she'd agreed to be his wife, he didn't feel the need to rush things. He had the rest of his life to make love to her, and he was going to enjoy savoring every second of their time together.

She trailed her fingers down the length of his arms and back up again, lifting her hips to meet him. "You're insatiable," she teased.

"Only for you, baby." Brett slipped his tongue into her mouth and then slipped his cock into her pussy.

She moaned into his mouth, but he didn't release her lips. He liked the feel and sound of her moans against his lips and tongue. Brett reached down and put one hand on her waist, pinning her to the bed. But he didn't increase his speed at all.

"Brett," she whimpered, wiggling her hips, writhing against him. "Please, I need more. I want you to fuck me."

He raised a brow and grinned. "Oh yeah?"

God, he loved it when she talked like that, when she told him exactly what she wanted and how she wanted it. Brett pulled out of her and kneeled between her legs. He grabbed her hips and pulled her so that her ass and thighs were resting on his. Then he shoved his cock into her with one hard thrust.

"Like this?" His movements were relentless, hard, determined.

"Yes!" Her screams encouraged him, and he fucked her so hard he was surprised she didn't tell him to stop. Amy clutched his arms, her nails scratching him as she did. "Oh God, yeah, that's..." Her words were lost as her orgasm tore through her.

"Fuck, Amy, so tight." Christ, her pussy got unbearably tight every time she came.

Brett brought his body forward so that her legs were bent and her knees rested on her shoulders. His hands were on either side of her head, and he kissed her just as hard as he fucked her. The feel of his balls slapping against her with each forward thrust was slowly weakening his control – not that he had much left to begin with, but he was definitely losing it.

"More," he muttered incoherently. Despite being as far in her as he could physically get, it wasn't enough. It would never be enough.

Brett released her lips and flung his head back, closing his eyes and letting out a sound that was animalistic, laced with pure, undiluted pleasure. His cock jerked inside of her as he came. Then he collapsed on top of her, unable to breathe, think, move. Since they'd started having sex, he'd had some pretty intense orgasm, but nothing like the one he'd just had. It drained him.

"I didn't hurt you, did I?" he mumbled into her neck.

"No," she said breathlessly, stroking the back of his neck. "That was amazing."

He kissed her neck and eased out of her. The sight of her post-coital, sated, sleepy... God, how had he almost missed this? Missed her? Being with her? Loving her? When he allowed himself to think about how close he'd come to never having her, it clutched at his heart.

"Hey, what's wrong?" she asked with a concerned look.

"Nothing." He smiled. "I was just thinking about how much I love you." Rolling onto his back, he brought Amy to him, tucking her tight to his side. "After last night, I'm pretty sure they already know, but I want to go to my parents and tell them about us, about the engagement."

"Really?" Her eyes sparked with excitement.

He laughed. "Yes. Besides, I'm going to have to explain sooner or later why I'm not living in my apartment anymore."

"That's true." She draped her arm over his stomach and hugged him.

Brett kissed the top of her head and closed his eyes. Even though he couldn't see her, he could feel her. "Why are you staring at me?" he asked.

"I've just never seen you look so relaxed."

"That's because I've never been this relaxed before." They'd spent more time having sex than they did sleeping, and it was finally starting to catch up with him. "I love you, baby," he whispered as sleep overcame him.

Brett squeezed Amy's hand as he opened the front door to his parents' house. "Ready for this?" he asked.

She took a deep breath. "Yes."

Together, they walked inside and were immediately greeted by his mother. She stood in the foyer, arms crossed, and a displeased look on her face. But then her gaze lowered to where Brett held Amy's hand firmly in his.

Ginny smiled. "Which one of you is going to explain?"

Without releasing Amy's hand, he took a step forward and gave his mother a kiss on the cheek. "I'm sorry I snapped at you the other night, Mom."

"And I'm sorry I stormed out of here the way I did," Amy said.

Ginny nodded. "Apologies accepted."

"Are Dad and Craig here? There's something we need to tell everyone."

"They're out back." Ginny turned on her heel and escorted Brett and Amy through the house and into the backyard.

Dad and Craig were seated at the patio table engrossed in a game of cards. Mom took a seat and motioned for them to do the same. Brett cleared his throat. It was now or never. He knew the moment the words were out of his mouth, his mother would go into planning mode. But that was okay, because the sooner he could make Amy his wife, the better.

He took a deep breath, and then said, "Amy and I are getting married."

Both his mother and father jerked their heads up to look at them. Craig didn't even flinch. "What?" Ginny said, standing.

"I asked Amy to marry me, and she said yes," Brett said.

"But...how...I mean, I thought...you two have never even dated," Ginny sputtered.

Brett laughed. "No, not really, but I realized on my honeymoon that Amy is the woman I'm supposed to be with. We've known each other our entire lives, Mom."

"You're not going to leave him at the altar, too, are you?" Craig said with a chuckle.

"Craig!" his father admonished.

"I wouldn't dream of it," Amy said.

And that's when Ginny finally lost it. She flung her arms around Amy and cried with joy. "Oh, Amy, dear, welcome to the family, officially." She released Amy and turned to Brett, smacking him on the arm. "It took you long enough."

Brett smiled. Ginny definitely reacted better to this engagement announcement than she had to his previous one. His father stood and enveloped him in a hug, whispering congratulations. Brett stood and watched as Amy and his mom talked about the wedding. Amy's smile lit up his life, made him feel happier than he'd ever felt. And she was all his. Now. Forever.

"Okay, this calls for a celebration," Ginny said, clapping her hands. "Dean, go to the cellar and get a bottle of champagne. I'll go get the glasses."

Brett pulled out a chair and sat next to Craig. Amy walked over and sat on Brett's lap and wrapped her arms around his neck. He nuzzled her and whispered, "Are you happy, baby?"

She smiled. "I've never been happier."

He framed her face with his hands and kissed her softly. "I love you," he said against her lips.

"Love you, too," she whispered back, and then engaged him in another kiss.

Craig groaned. "Get a room."

Amy laughed, but she didn't get off Brett's lap. "Oh, Craig, it's okay. You'll find someone, too."

"Yeah, I know." Craig grinned.

"I hear Amy's sister is single again," Brett said, putting his arms around Amy's waist and massaging her lower hip.

"Lucy?" Craig asked.

Amy gently elbowed Brett. "Don't play matchmaker."

"Yes, dear." He winked.

Brett was starting to wish he'd told his parents over the phone instead of coming here in person because he'd do just about anything right now to be alone with Amy. He craved her worse than a drug addict craved drugs. She was his undoing.

Chapter Twenty-Three

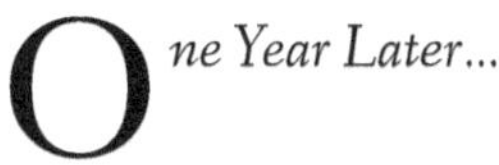

"Are you sure you want to do this?" Craig whispered, playfully nudging Brett with his shoulder.

"I've never been surer of anything in my life," Brett responded as he looked around.

He was back on Tri Pinnae Island, back on the secluded beach where he'd first told Amy he'd loved her. Only this time, he was surrounded by his parents, his brother, and Amy's sister. And he was standing beneath a flower arch, waiting for Amy to walk down the aisle toward him, toward their future together.

This island was where they'd found each other, so they'd agreed it was where they'd vow their love to each other, too. And it couldn't have been more perfect. Brett had even managed to get the same exact bungalow they'd stayed in last time. Their family was staying all the way on the other side of the island, giving Brett and Amy a little bit of privacy.

"It's not too late to call this off," Craig teased.

Brett laughed. "Not a chance in hell." He turned to look at his brother. "In fact, you'll probably have to hold me back so I don't run down that aisle and grab her."

Craig flung his head back and laughed. "You've got it bad."

Yes, he did, but he didn't care. The small island band began to play, and Brett's heart momentarily stopped. This was it. He clutched his hands in front of him and twisted them, his nerves getting the best of him. Blowing out a breath, he tried to calm himself. This was Amy – his best friend, the love of his life – she would walk down that aisle. She would.

And then she did.

Brett couldn't stop smiling. God, she was beautiful. Dressed in a knee length white dress, sandals, and a large flower tucked behind her ear, she was absolutely stunning. She stole his breath and his heart all over again. It felt like it took forever for her to finally reach him, but when she did, he took both of her hands into his and looked into her eyes. She smiled at him, and he swore his knees were going to give out.

"I understand you've written your own vows?" said the man who was officiating over the wedding.

"Yes." Brett's voice was barely above a whisper.

He cleared his throat, not remembering a time in his life when he'd been this nervous. Nothing about their relationship was normal so they'd opted for a very non-traditional wedding. Amy gently squeezed his hands, and he licked his lips.

"Go ahead," the man said.

Brett nodded and refocused his gaze on his bride. "You are the one person in the world I've always been able to count on. I've spent my life choosing you over all others, and today I stand here, once again choosing you. I choose you to be my best friend, my wife, my lover, and my forever. Finding you was a dream come true, and I vow to spend the rest of my life making all your dreams come true." He paused and noticed the tears in her eyes. Brett reached up and gently wiped them away. "You have made me the happiest man in the world, and I'm going to devote every second of every day making you as happy as you've made me. I love you, Amy King, so much."

Amy reached up and wiped away more tears. Then she smiled. Exhaling, she said, "Wow, okay..."

He rubbed his thumbs over her knuckles in an attempt to calm her.

She nodded and then spoke. "As my friend, you've always been there for me, given me a shoulder to cry on. You make me laugh like no one else can, and you drive me crazy, too." She chuckled. "But I love you. I've loved you since the day we met, and I will love you until the day I die. You're my best friend, my soul mate, and my husband. I can't wait to start spending the rest of our lives together."

"The rings," the man said.

Brett took the ring that Craig held and slipped it onto Amy's finger. "I love you," he said.

Amy took the ring from her sister and put it on Brett's finger. "I love you," she whispered, her tears once again streaking down her cheeks.

"I now pronounce you husband and wife. You may kiss the bride."

Brett wasted no time pulling Amy into his arms and kissing her. He parted her lips with his tongue and twisted his tongue around, over, and under hers. She moaned softly, and he forced himself to pull away, to remember that they were standing in front of their family. He was so looking forward to later, when they were alone. Brett would show her just how much he really loved her.

Amy was now officially Mrs. Brett Hudson, and she hadn't stopped smiling all day. Now that the ceremony was over, they were having a small, private celebration in one of the dining rooms located in the hotel restaurant. The band that had played during the wedding was now playing for the entire place.

Brett held her in his arms as they danced, totally oblivious to everything and everyone around them. "So, tell me, Mrs. Hudson, is there anything you'd like to do while we're here this time?" Brett kissed her lips.

"I really like the sound of that...Mrs. Hudson." She smiled.

"Mmm, me too." He spun her around and pulled her back into his arms. "But you didn't answer my question."

"Aside from making love to my husband every chance I get? Let me see..." She pretended to think about what she wanted to do, but she knew. "I want to give you a present."

He stopped moving for a moment and raised a brow. "A present?"

"Yeah." Now that she'd said it, her stomach flopped.

Maybe now, here, wasn't the best time to give him this gift. But, damn, she'd been waiting for weeks for this, and she couldn't possibly wait a moment longer. She'd intentionally waited until their wedding day to give him this particular gift.

"Okay." He laughed. "What is it?"

Amy pulled him closer and put her mouth near his ear. "We're going to have a baby, Brett. I'm pregnant."

Brett jerked his head back so that he was looking at her face. She held her breath, waiting for him to respond. Since they'd been together, they hadn't really talked about having kids, so she really didn't know how he was going to react, but she hoped it was positive.

Slowly, Brett's lips curved into a smile. "I'm going to be a dad?" he whispered as if he didn't fully believe her.

"Yes."

"I'm going to be a dad!" He picked her up and spun her around. "God, Amy...wow...I..." Brett crushed his mouth over hers. "I love you so damn much."

Amy sighed with relief and was overcome with emotion. "Thank you, Brett, for everything. For loving me, marrying me, giving me a baby..." Her words were lost to her tears.

Never, in a million years, did she think she'd ever be this happy. But because of Brett, she was, and she'd do whatever it took to make sure they both stayed this happy. Forever.

Thank you for taking the time to read *JILTED*. If you have a moment, could you please leave a review on your favorite retailer, Goodreads, and/or Bookbub? A review doesn't need to be more than a sentence or two, and they are the best way to help an author.

**KEEP READING for a
SNEAK PEEK at
NOAH: My Best Friend's Father, Book 1
AVAILABLE NOW!**

LEXI LAWTON
MY BEST FRIEND'S FATHER
Noah

Sneak Peek: Noah

I loosened my tie and rolled the tension from my shoulders. When I'd started Abrams Design and Construction, I'd done so because I wanted to work with my hands, build things from the ground up. I never anticipated how much time and effort I'd have to put into schmoozing clients. It was hands-down the worst part of my job. But it was also the one part of my job that gave me the big fat paychecks I'd become accustomed to.

"I'm home," I called as I let myself into the house. I dropped my briefcase on the foyer table and toed off my shoes. "Heather?"

"In here, Dad," she said from the kitchen.

I smiled. Now that my only daughter was a freshman in college, I never knew when or if she'd be home. The nights she stayed on campus late, this big house was lonely and as quiet as a cemetery. I walked into the kitchen to find her at the table, books sprawled out in front of her.

"Hey, pumpkin." I ruffled her hair like I used to do when she was little, and she swatted my hand away.

"I ordered take-out from Mariano's. Should be here soon."

"Sounds good." I grabbed a beer from the refrigerator, twisted off the top, and took a long pull.

"How'd the pitch go?" Heather leaned back in her chair and stretched her arms over her head.

"We made the sale. We'll spend the next two weeks going over blueprints and then construction will start next month." Setting my beer down, I removed my tie and tossed it on the counter. "I hate wearing those damn things."

Heather laughed. "You should wear them more often. You look nicer when you're not in tattered jeans and covered in dirt."

Shaking my head, I took another drink. "Hey, watch it. That dirt is what's paying for your college." I tilted my beer bottle in her direction. "What're you working on?"

She scrunched up her face and stuck out her tongue. "My final project for my business class and studying for final exams."

Pride swelled inside of me. I never had any expectations that Heather would take over the construction company I'd built, but when she said she wanted to go to college for business so she could learn the ins and outs and someday take over the family business, I didn't argue. If that's truly what she wanted, I wouldn't stand in her way.

I finished my beer and set the bottle in the sink. "I'm going to grab a quick shower and change before dinner gets here."

She mumbled her acknowledgement, her face buried in her books. Damn, I was proud of that kid. I headed toward the stairs when there was a knock on the door. Dinner couldn't be here already, could it? I reached for the doorknob when the door swung open, and in walked Corrine Tate.

Tall. Thin. Curves in all the right places. Long hair that begged to be grabbed. Big, innocent eyes. She was my daughter's best friend.

And my greatest temptation.

"Oh, sorry, Mr. Abrams." Corrine smiled sheepishly. "I didn't hit you, did I?"

"No." I stepped back. "C'mon in."

She entered, and I closed the door behind her. When I turned to face her, I immediately noticed two things. First, she was wearing a very thin tank top with a bra that pushed her tits up into delectable mounds of tanned flesh that I wanted to bury my face in. I shifted on my feet, hoping the erection I felt coming on wouldn't alert her to the nasty thoughts racing through my mind.

Second, she had two bags with her—one backpack stuffed full of books, and her overnight bag. As Heather's closest friend, Corrine had been spending the night here since she was twelve, and she always brought the same purple bag. I didn't care that she spent the night, but knowing she was here, only a couple doors down from my room was a temptation that was becoming increasingly hard to ignore.

Ever since Corrine had turned eighteen a year and a half ago, I hadn't been able to deny my growing attraction to her. She was a beautiful young woman. Smart. Funny. Dripping with sex appeal. And I wanted her in the worst fucking way possible. Too bad I was literally old enough to be her father.

"Looking good, Mr. A.," she said, interrupting my thoughts.

My eyes widened, and my heart slammed against my ribs. "What?"

She swirled her finger up and down the length of my body. "The suit. It looks good on you."

"Oh." I glanced down at my clothes. "Yeah, I had a sales pitch today. I was just going to go change."

She pouted, and I crossed my arms so I wouldn't yank her body to mine and suck on that full, luscious bottom lip that she'd stuck out. My cock strained behind my zipper, demanding to be set free, to sink into her hot, young body.

"That's too bad. It looks good on you." She smiled, her emerald-green eyes lighting up her face.

For half a second, I considered leaving the suit on, for her. But that was a silly fantasy I couldn't entertain.

"Heather and I have to study for finals." They attended the local university together, but Corrine was enrolled in a liberal arts program because she was unsure what she wanted to do with her life. She was, as she liked to say, "exploring her options."

I'd give my left fucking nut to explore her. I nodded. "She's in the kitchen."

"Thanks." She spun on her heel and headed out of the foyer.

Her short shorts barely covered her ass cheeks, and I couldn't help but watch her walk away, the sway of her hips teasing me. I swore she dressed like that on purpose, like she was hoping to get a rise out of me. Little did she know, it worked. Every. Fucking. Time. I blew out a breath and turned to go upstairs when there was another knock on the door. Christ, it was like a circus around here tonight.

I opened the door, and the delivery boy from Mariano's stood there, holding three large bags. "Delivery for Heather Abrams."

"Yep." I pulled my wallet out of my back pocket. "How much?"

"Oh, uh, thirty-six forty-two."

"Is that the food?" Heather came racing through the foyer and then came to a complete stop. "Hey, Bryan."

"Hi, Heather." His cheeks turned pink, and I scowled.

"I got this, Dad." She took the two twenties from my hand and nudged me out of the way.

As much as I wanted to lock her up in her room and never let her think about guys, let alone be with one, I could take a hint. Dragging a hand through my hair, I retreated to the kitchen. I froze.

Corrine was bent over in the fridge, ass on full display. Momentarily closing my eyes, I took a deep breath, but my cock was already rock hard, and that view wasn't making it any softer. The tank top she wore barely reached the waistband of her shorts, leaving a sliver of her back exposed. My gaze lingered on that spot as I imagined dragging my lips across her flesh; then my eyes lowered to her hips.

I flexed my fingers, dying to know how my hands would feel on her hips, grabbing them as I slid my hard cock in and out of her. I adjusted myself. From this angle, it appeared as though she weren't wearing panties. Fuck that was hot. She straightened and turned around. My eyes snapped up to her face.

"Thought you were changing," she said, closing the fridge and twisting the top off a bottle of water. "Not that I'm complaining or anything."

"I was, but the food is here."

She looked around as if she didn't believe me.

"Heather's out there flirting with the delivery boy." I frowned.

Corrine laughed. "Ah, yes. Bryan. She sorta has a thing for him."

"I noticed."

"Aw, don't worry, Mr. A." She stepped up to me and patted my chest. The touch sent a shiver through me and caused my dick to twitch with need. "Bryan's a good guy."

"No one will ever be good enough for my daughter." I nearly snarled the words.

Corrine's hand fell away from my chest, trailing down my stomach before she pulled away completely. I immediately missed the feel of her hand on me, even if it was an innocent touch. "She's lucky to have someone who cares so much."

My heart squeezed. Corrine's father was a prick who cared more about work than his own family. And her mother was always too busy fucking anyone with a dick who would give her a second look. That's why Corrine spent so much time here, so she could get away from her messed up parents. And I was more than happy to accommodate her.

"Hey." I took her hand into mine, rubbing my thumb over her knuckles. Her hand was so small and delicate compared to mine, her skin silky soft. "There's no one out there good enough for you, either."

Not even me, although I would never hurt her like some of the other assholes she'd encounter during her life. I would worship her, protect her, always be there for her.

"Thank you." She closed the distance between us, her chest rubbing against mine with each breath she took.

My shirt did nothing to hide how hard her nipples were, and I suppressed a groan. *She's only nineteen. She's my daughter's best friend.* I repeated the mantra, but it wasn't having the same effect it normally did.

"That means a lot," she whispered.

I gave her hand a squeeze then released it before I did something stupid. Like bend her over the counter, yank those shorts down around her ankles, and shove my cock so deep inside her she wouldn't know where she ended and I started.

"Well, it's the truth." My voice was deeper than usual and raspy.

She rose up on her tiptoes and pressed her lips to my cheek, dangerously close to my lips. This was not the first time she'd kissed my cheek—far from it—but this time was different. Electric. She lingered as if she wanted me to turn my head a fraction of an inch and meet her lips. And God damn if I wasn't contemplating doing just that. It would be so easy.

"Corrine, honey."

She smelled like coconuts and the beach. Instinctively, I slid my arm around her waist and drew her closer. She was all soft curves and luscious warmth, a stark contrast to how hard every part of my body was, and there was no way she didn't feel my erection pressed against her.

I knew I should care. I should pull away, try to hide my arousal, but a part of me—that sick, twisted part of me that I tried to keep buried—wanted her to know how I felt when she was around.

"Got the food," Heather said as she entered the kitchen. "I don't know about you two, but I'm starving."

Corrine jerked away abruptly and cleared her throat. Without a word or glance in my direction, she stepped around me. *Shit.* I'd crossed the line and made her uncomfortable. I was such a dickhead. Any crazy notions I had about her, about being with her, had to remain locked up tight in my mind. An unattainable fantasy and nothing more.

BUY NOW!

195

About the Author

Born and raised in Central New York, Lexi Lawton is an only child who found companionship in books. When she was old enough to put pen to paper, she began writing her own stories of love, suspense, and heartbreak.

Today, Lexi lives in Michigan with her husband, a herd of kids, and what could probably be considered a zoo of dogs, cats, and fish. She secretly thrives on the chaos. To stay up to date on what Lexi is doing, check out her website: www.lexilawtonauthor.weebly.com.

Free Book!

Want to snag a copy of *Christmas Confessions* for FREE?

Sign up for Lexi's newsletter and download your copy now!

Other Books by Lexi:

<u>COLLINS BROTHERS SERIES:</u>

Trusting Tanner

Chasing Xander

<u>HARMONY FALLS UNIVERSITY SERIES:</u>

Obligation

Obsession

<u>MY BEST FRIEND'S FATHER SERIES:</u>

Noah

Darian

Ryan